NEW DIRECTIONS 33

In memoriam
HEINZ HENGHES
1906–1975

Heinz Henghes's drawing of a centaurlike figure, which appears on the title page of this book, was originally made at Rapallo, in the early 1930s, for a marble sculpture now in the collection of the Agnelli family. The design was adopted in 1937 as the New Directions colophon and continues to be reproduced on the title page and jacket casing of every number of *New Directions in Prose and Poetry.*

"Heinz Henghes, the sculptor, died on December 20 in Bordeaux," *The Times* of London wrote in its obituary notice last year. "In him, European sculpture has lost a versatile artist and an endearing, eccentric character.

"Born in Hamburg in 1906, Henghes ran away from home while still in his teens to try his luck in the United States. It was not until 1922, following a meeting with Isamu Noguchi, that he turned seriously to sculpture, for poetry had been his first ambition. Indeed, it was some early published verses which had caught the eye of Ezra Pound that led to his leaving New York in 1932 to settle at Pound's invitation, in Rapallo in Italy, where he soon made his mark and name, an early patron being Renato Wild, who later commissioned Henghes to decorate with his marble birdlike sculptures a swimming pool at the Villa Rospini on Lake Como.

"However, the nomad in Henghes soon took him from Italy to Switzerland and in 1937 on to London, where in the following year he had two one-man shows at the Guggenheim and the St. George's galleries. The war turned him into an air raid warden, a broadcaster, and a British subject, and he stayed in England until 1953, exhibiting at the Hanover and Piccadilly galleries and teaching for a spell in the early 1950s at the Royal College of Art under Frank Dobson. From 1953 to 1964, he worked and lived in the Dordogne, exhibiting in Paris, London, New York, and Frankfurt. He returned to England in 1964, becoming head of the sculpture department of the Winchester School of Art until his retirement, when he went back to the Dordogne as a much-loved figure in the little commune of Tursac. . . ."

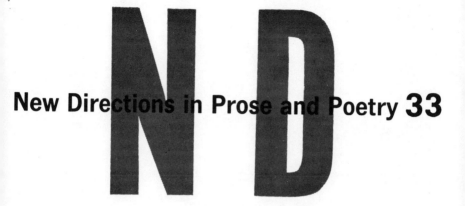

New Directions in Prose and Poetry 33

Edited by J. Laughlin

with Peter Glassgold and Frederick R. Martin

A New Directions Book

ACKNOWLEDGMENTS

Grateful acknowledgment is made to the editors and publishers of books and magazines where some of the selections in this volume first appeared: for Walter Abish, *Fiction International* (Copyright © 1975 by Joe David Bellamy); for Martin Bax, *Ambit* (London); for Christine Brooke-Rose, *Thru* (Hamish Hamilton, Ltd., London); for Frederick Busch, *The New Review* (London, Copyright © 1975 by Frederick Busch); for M. D. Elevitch, *Lillabulero* (Copyright © 1974 by M. D. Elevitch); for Aram Saroyan, *The New York Times* (Copyright © 1975 by Aram Saroyan).

Manufactured in the United States of America
First published clothbound (ISBN: 0–8112–0616–5) and as New Directions Paperbook 419 (ISBN: 0–8112–0617–3) in 1976
Published simultaneously in Canada by McClelland & Stewart, Ltd.

New Directions Books are published for James Laughlin
by New Directions Publishing Corporation,
333 Sixth Avenue, New York 10014

CONTENTS

FOUR UNCOLLECTED POEMS

THOMAS MERTON

PAPER CRANES

(The Hibakusha come to Gethsemani)

How can we tell a paper bird
Is stronger than a hawk
When it has no metal for talons?
It needs no power to kill
Because it is not hungry.

Wilder and wiser than eagles
It ranges round the world
Without enemies
And free of cravings.

The child's hand
Folding these wings
Wins no wars and ends them all.

Thoughts of a child's heart
Without care, without weapons!
So the child's eye
Gives life to what it loves
Kind as the innocent sun
And lovelier than all dragons!

COMEDY CARD FOR A SERIOUS CASE

No smoke says law light-
Ning arrest alarm for
Thunder torpedo smells oxygen sub-
Marine warn tender sinker
Thousands envy dead

Warn unwelcome torpedo
(Smell oxygen)
Warn alert alone
Well careful pilot treads to land's end horizon:
Falls one match and striking the lightning dead

Slow sunboat goes by under an inventive bed
Rocksplit trumpet for laughing carload in the pit of souls
How clear the matching joker dies of reward!
Poor old vaudeville smoker, without an oath
Over and over down comedy canyon.

Bed is no safe engine in electric doom
As Daddy rides the sunbuilt air
Flashes in jet jokes
How he can swear!
His wits are all gone down the corridor
Or in the sunboat under Pharaoh's electric bed
Gone gone with the despairing breast
Stroke of the dead

So Spring bolt clarion hails expensive blood
Careful pilot steers away on tall-aired flood
And all the oxygen is good for chain volts
Drives Death boat down coronary night

So Daddy rides
(And lends light-)
Ning better than Ben Hur's
Sightless fates,
A roaring winner
In a legendary race.

SOLITARY LIFE

White-collar man blue-collar
Man I am a no-collar man
(least of all a *Roman* collar!)
Shave twice a week
Maybe.

Hear the trains out there
Two miles away
Trucks too
The road not near.

Hear the owls in the wood and pray
When I can
I don't talk
About all that
What is there to say?

Yes, I had beer in this place
A while back and once
Whiskey.

And I worry about the abbot
Coming up here to
Inspect
And finding
A copy of *Newsweek*
Under the bed.

Now it's another
Morning and the doves
Boom softly and the world
Goes on it seems
Forever.

LETTERS TO CHE: CANTO BILINGUE

Te escribo cartas, Che,
En la sazon de lluvias
Envenenadas

They came without faces
Found you with eyeless rays
The tin grasshoppers
With five cornered magic
Wanting to feed you
To the man-eating computer

Te escribo cartas, Guerrero,
Vestido de hojas y lunas

But you won and became
The rarest jungle tree
A lost leopard
Out of metal's way

Te escribo cartas
Hermano invisible
Gato de la noche lejana

Cat of far nights
Whisper of a Bolivian kettle
Cry
Of an Inca hill

Te escribo cartas, Niño,
De la musica callada.

GEORGE DOLBY

Or, The Cannibal Sheep

FREDERICK BUSCH

He said "Really, Dolby, I don't *want* to sleep in any more towns named Utica. Utica. *Utica.* Doesn't it sound like an herb you take for your health?" He rubbed the side of his face which possibly didn't function—I doubted if he felt his fingers—and he sighed. Long moist sigh. "Perhaps it would help."

Because he needed some. Because he was the whore of self-pity, and also brave. He was the Chief. And what he saw—I calculate this, I'm guessing only a bit, I all but wiped his arse so many days and nights—was the right-hand side, just that, of any signs he claimed to read out whole. The feeling was dead, the vision crippled, his left leg dragged enough to make the carpets whisper. When he didn't know we looked, and maybe when he did, it seemed as though his blood beat. But when he was on the stage he was a decorated panther, and he stalked, all giant eyes all-seeing, and hunger ready to spring. And he was tender, when he wished, as children asleep. The stage was his mind.

On the train sometimes he wore a gutta-percha overshoe on the left foot, claiming that a lingering touch of frostbite had swollen the toes. He never admitted to us he was ill. Sometimes he said he was exhausted, but never mortal, like men. When he wore the huge shoe, along with some pink silk waistcoat, his vanity kept him from the corridors of the railroad car; so I never sat, was always running his errands, opening windows, wiping the foul brown spit of some tobacco-chewing American traveler with a handkerchief he'd give me, then tell me to throw away.

Where does one deposit excremental cloths on a passenger train attempting to derail itself in New England or New York? No matter. Dolby will do it. Dolby will open the window so the Chief won't suffer from excessive heat—"My God, Dolby, they don't breathe *air!* They live in steam. They're orchids. Which rarely are watered. And spit tobacco juice."—and Dolby will fetch the trainman to move offensive passengers so the Chief will be surrounded by a wall of empty seats. And Dolby will listen when the Chief clears his throat, pressing the dead left side, rubs his pouter-pigeon chest, says "D-Dolby, it is the True American." Meaning—he loved his phrases better than the crowds who queued for days to hear him read from books they'd read before—that he had what he called the True American Catarrh. Meaning, too, that Dolby sometimes stammered when he spoke, that his affliction unnerved the big bald arranger of bookings, meals, even toilet-cleanings, and that the Chief found Dolby's difficulties amusing. Mouse in the paws of his language.

From Liverpool I came, on the loathsome boat. To meet with Osgood and Fields, who treated Osgood, his employee, like a son. To arrange first with Fields for the redistribution of books in cities where the Chief would read, and then to travel with Osgood, rocketing back and forth in trains and often carriages, estimating audiences, booking the halls, drinking bourbon whisky—my Lord!—with ignorant journalists, sending wires home about America's love for the Chief. Then back to Boston while Osgood, mediocre assistant, returned to England to fetch the Chief.

Osgood said he was often gone from his quarters during the passage. Osgood, because he is stupid, said the Chief paced the decks and thought of his absent wife. Never. His wife had been absent longer than the public knew. His wife was dead to him for years. And it wasn't Ellen Ternan he thought of, either, though at night I wager he rubbed his body in her name. I wonder if he ever rubbed hers. No, he was belowdecks. I saw this while I dined in Boston with fools and rich men's servants. I lay on the coverlet and smoked cigars and saw him, bilious with the motion and the rancid air, standing in the cargo hold he'd ordered opened to him, rocking in the *Cuba* and in his giant mind, staring in half-light at the stand and screen, the platform his daughter had given him, and the gas-lighting apparatus he'd insisted on loading himself. Staring at the gas pipes. Seeing flames.

"He is as tender as a woman and as watchful as a doctor" is what he wrote about me. He left his letters for me to seal and post. Scraps of his imagination. Everything changed by his pen to what he thought it should be. I didn't recognize the incidents he wrote of, often. Because America, the reading tour, Kate the soft wife he'd thrown away, her sister Georgina Hogarth who stayed to care for his children in his home, the actress he sealed in apartments and paid for, the years of 1867–68, and Dolby, who stammered —"Whenever," he wrote, "the name Cambridge, that rock ahead in his speech, appeared in the itinerary"—all were in his mind. He was a pirate, he stole the living world.

That snowy mustache, and the visible pain, his monstrous strength when he whipped the weeping audiences—Little Nell's noisome dying, the wretched Paul Dombey in his mystical transports—and his letters to and about himself: "I cannot remember to whom I wrote last, but it will not much matter if I make a mistake, this being generally to report myself." And then, making me laugh and love him like a slave: "For now, farewell. My desk and I have just arisen from the floor."

In the Parker House, where he staggered in the hallway at the start of the tour, December 1867, bleating that the heat of hallways made him faint, we sat in the dining room surrounded by white linen and threatened by an avalanche of crystal. He tapped a hard roll against his goblet—he was nibbling at partridge, too ill even then to taste his food—and he said "Dolby, the Negroes."

"Sir?"

"Where are the Negroes?"

"I see only Irishmen. Only Irishmen wait on table at the Parker, sir. This is Boston."

"Yes." He prodded the carcass of the bird with his bread. "All the servants are Irish—willing, but not able. You want a black man for the right service of a meal."

And that night the man who had taxed America for slavery wrote to Cartwright in London "The old, untidy, incapable, lounging, shambling black serves you as a free man. Free of course he ought to be; but the stupendous absurdity of making him a voter glares out of every roll of his eye, stretch of his mouth, and bump of his head. I have a strong impression that the race must fade out of the States very fast. It never can hold its own against a striving, restless, shifty people." He made up the entire earth!

Next morning, paler, and over the queasiness we'd both complained of, he called me into the sitting room of his suite where he sat erect at the writing table, eyes bright with ink. I took a letter to post to Miss Hogarth. And wondered when he told the truth. "Dolby has been twice poisoned, and Osgood once. When the snow is deep upon the ground, and the partridges cannot get their usual food, they eat something (I don't know what, if anybody does) which does not poison *them*, but which poisons the people who eat them. The symptoms, which last some twelve hours, are violent sickness, cold perspiration, and the formation of some detestable mucus in the stomach. You may infer that partridges have been banished from our bill of fare.

"Did I tell you that the severity of the weather, and the heat of the intolerable furnaces, dry the hair and break the nails of strangers. Dolby watches me brush my hair which then falls out; then he gasps to see me coming apart; then rushes to my side. He is always going about with an immense bundle that looks like a sofa cushion but is in reality paper money; and always works like a Trojan."

Yes. And is often as full of spearheads and barbs. As in Providence, when the unstoppable ticket speculators had charged more than four times our price, and a crowd halted me at the hotel and I thought I'd be hanged on the spot. Inside, that evening, he said "Indispensable Dolby. Good Dolby!"

But he was the capable one. Arriving at the theater, interviewing the man who would control the gas—he always spends inordinate time with gas men—and then, in a small room back of the stage, his face as white with pain as his mustache was with fifty-six years, sitting in the most arctic silence over a small meal, never eating it, never, then sending for an egg beaten up in sherry. Never speaking. Holding his prompt copies, not looking at them ever, before he walked on stage. Sending me or Osgood or one of the others to look at the size and quality of his audience. Then, suddenly, as if I had asked him: "Generally, Dolby, they are very good audiences indeed. Don't you think? Granted, they do not perceive touches of art to *be* art. But they're responsive to the broad results of the touches. I can't ask for more."

"No, sir. They love you."

"Love! I'm here for money, not love. The Inimitable does it for dollars, convertible to guineas. I've a house full of children to see to, you know that."

"Yes, sir. Of course, the money."

"Yes."

Then a grimace as he moved his foot back and leaned his palms on his thighs. "My God, do you remember poor Longfellow?"

"I've never met anyone braver, sir. One couldn't tell, from speaking with him. That—"

"No. I knew, of course. I would have known. The horror, it was still in his eyes."

"I hadn't the opportunity to dine with him."

"Good Dolby. No, you were rushing about, carting all those crackling American dollars. Did you sleep last night?"

"A bit, sir. The journalists—"

"Why must they call me *Charlie?* As if we chewed tobacco together in some frontier saloon. *Charlie!*"

"They presume, sir. They slapped my back all night. It's quite sore."

"You do serve, Dolby." He drank his sherry and curled his fine nose. It was pale at the bridge. "And they asked about my wife? They questioned you about my—friends at home?"

"They're curious, sir. They would write about your gold studs— they do. They would write about anything."

"Write! They *pen.* None of them can write."

"True. They pen on, though. About anything."

"You told them—of course not. You were Dolby, weren't you?"

"Yes, sir. And still am."

The smile, and then its death, his dramatic faraway stare. "Yes, imagine Longfellow, still living there, in the same old house where that beautiful wife of his burned. I thought I still smelled the smoke when his cook brought in the roast. I couldn't get the scene out of my imagination. She was in a blaze in an instant, rushed into his arms with a wild cry, and never spoke afterwards." Then: "I ought to be alone now, don't you think?"

And then, with no limp or frailty, the mounting of the stage as if it were a cliff he dared to look down from. And, starting softly with Bob Sawyer's party, and a gracious utterly insincere comment or two, and then David Copperfield, he squeezed them by the throat until they roared to be squeezed harder. More sherry with egg between the parts. Silent sitting, perspiration and gauntness over him as if he were stone sprayed by a waterfall. And then back before them and—they were before *him,* performed for him at his command and never knew it—Nancy's murder by Sikes. When he cried "No!" in his grainy falsetto, a woman with a pearl collar shrieked back "No! No!" and young Kelly, always eager to be used by any of us, led her gently to the auditorium door. She wept on him. The Chief didn't pause, though he was grateful to her, I know.

So, on. Coughing from two or three in the morning until dawn— loudly enough for me to hear next door, and suffer on his behalf —and then less sleep, and tasting nothing, eating nearly not at all, taking laudanum for relief of the "frostbite," becoming more exhausted, more depressed. The incessant opening of windows, the complaints about lack of fresh air, the letters to everyone, as if their existence depended on what he said he saw, the America he invented.

When I brought him sherry in Albany, as he—what else?—wrote definitively of the city he'd visited twice ("a simulacrum of the western frontier" he decided to someone in London), he said "Do you remember when I visited the medical school in Boston, Dolby?"

"Yes, sir. You didn't speak much about it. Was it rewarding?"

"I saw where that extraordinary murder was done by that man Webster. You remember that I spoke of it."

"Yes, sir. The murder."

"Yes. There was the furnace, stinking horribly, as if all the dismembered pieces were still inside it." He was writing to *me.* "And there were all the grim spouts, and sinks, and chemical appliances. Ghastly. Fascinating. That was the night I dined with Longfellow. He is so dear."

"I believe he returns the favor with interest, sir."

"I flatter myself that he does. But what he told me—and after his own wife . . . He said he had dined with Webster less than a year before the murder, a party of ten or twelve. There they sat at their wine. Webster suddenly ordered the lights to be turned out, and a bowl of some burning mineral to be placed on the table. Longfellow telling stories with even a *spark* of fire in them! And in the weird light, all were horrified to see Webster with a rope around his neck! Holding it up, over the bowl, with his head jerked on one side, and his tongue lolled out, representing a man being hanged! Poking into his life and character, I find he was always a cruel man."

Yrs sincerely, etc.

"Dolby hardly ever dines," he writes to his daughter. "He is always tearing about at unreasonable hours. He works very hard." Yes. And sometimes wonders if he will require a restraining jacket or a hospital ward for the Chief—which first? The night in New York City, when he smelled smoke and it turned out that a part of the roof was on fire: the dancing and jigging! the drool and little cries! rushing to gather everything into his pockets, including a face rag from his bathroom! He said to himself, as if it were a child's song, "Fire. Fire. We're on fire." I soothed him, at last. He cannot tolerate awfully much of the world.

"I took charge at once" he writes to Miss Hogarth. "I was not surprised, having smelled fire for two hours. I got Scott up directly, told him to pack the books and clothes for the readings first, dressed, and pocketed my jewels and papers, while Dolby stuffed himself out with money. After a little chopping and cutting with axes and handing about with water, the fire was confined to a dining room in which it had originated, and then everybody talked to everybody else, the ladies being particularly loquacious and cheerful. And so we got to bed again at about two. The excitement of the readings continues unabated, the tickets for readings are sold as soon as they are ready. Dolby continues to be the most unpopular man in America (mainly because he can't get four thousand people into a room that holds two thousand) and is reviled in print. Yesterday morning a newspaper proclaims of him: 'Surely it is time that the pudding-headed Dolby retired into the native gloom from which he has emerged.' He takes it very coolly."

Don't I? I carry the money in, then retire to the saloon bar where I tell the journalists what he wants them to know. We discuss him as the greatest literary figure of the age, and they agree, and I do too. He is. He invented the age. It's his book.

"Our hotel was on fire *again* the other night. But fires in this country are quite matters of course. There was a large one there at four this morning, and I don't think a single night has passed since I have been under the protection of the Eagle, but I have heard the fire bells dolefully clanging all over the city. Dolby sends his kindest regard. His hair has become quite white, the effect, I suppose, of the climate. He is so universally hauled over the coals. You may conceive what the low newspapers are here, when one of them yesterday morning had, as an item of news, the intelligence: 'The Readings. The chap calling himself Dolby got drunk last night, and was locked up in a police station for fighting an Irishman.' I don't find that anybody is shocked by this liveliness."

Some of this, I know, is in his mind. He will use it some time, so I may use it now. With a man like that, what's the difference between *as if* and *is?* Simply because he never gave me letters to Ellen Ternan, am I to imagine that he didn't write them? Part of his death-in-life was her absence, and his speculation—his constructing whole scenes and episodes—of her social activity in London. He never spoke of his wife. She and Thackeray had made trouble for him, despite his pained willingness to let her live in his house, sleeping alone in the room they shared while he slept in his newly renovated dressing room. She had borne ten children, and she had bored the Chief.

I think—I have a right to: I carried his cash and curried his coat—that he was drawn to Ternan, as he was drawn to America, because she was a fresh start. He never forgave America for not being innocent. He despaired of Ternan not only because she didn't love him (I knew this, always), but because once she was his, she was sullied. He needed love, he needed more than any man I knew. But he needed more to live forever in his mind. Ternan didn't want to live there.

Most of us did, or had to: as in New Haven, after I had discovered that the wretched Osgood, going on ahead, had been bribed by speculators to let them have great lots of tickets. "You know," the Chief said, "I'm a curious man. I conceived a terrible dislike to Osgood on board the *Cuba*, coming out. He was ill all the voyage, and I only saw him two or three times, staggering about the deck. But I underwent a change of feeling towards him, as if I had taken it in at the pores of the skin."

"He's dismissed, sir. And the Steinway Hall people have threatened to beat him nearly to death when he returns to New York."

"No, Dolby, we'll let him stay. *Now* he'll serve: he doesn't want the dragging into court I could give him. His limits will be narrow, and he'll touch no money again. But now that he'll serve as he should (I can guarantee it) we'll let him stay. He needs my protection. He'll work hard."

"The man's a criminal, sir."

"Who isn't? In the larger meaning."

"Of course."

So Osgood hated him then, and always, for the canny salvation. He was owned. But, to quote The Inimitable, who isn't? In February, back in Boston for another long engagement of readings, we found that President Johnson's impeachment had kept the audiences away. There were empty seats, and the Chief canceled the second week's readings: he hated empty seats. He thought to let his cough improve. How can mortality improve?

Restless in a lounge chair at the Parker—he was content only when he could complain of exhaustion—the Chief, then, announced to Osgood and me "My merry men, I am pleased to proclaim The Great International Walking Match. You'll enjoy it, I think. We can't sit idle for a week."

Osgood, smiling to his gums as always, asked him "Who's to run—er, walk, sir?"

"Good question, Osgood. You are perspicacious, you will rise. But first you will walk. You both will, I think. Won't you? A select audience of enraptured spectators, ladies fainting, the booming applause as the English Champion first cross the mark, swiveling his lithe b-body." I am not a small man. I do not parade myself, and I keep my overcoat buttoned. I looked at the carpeted floor and waited for Osgood to fawn.

I *heard* his skin stretch into smiles before he said "A pleasure, sir. I hope, though, to show you some American mettle."

"Such as you tried to collect, eh? Now *we* collect the American metal. Don't we, Dolby?"

"Yes, sir."

"You're the Man of Ross, Dolby. I think it's rather good. Osgood, you shall be the Boston Bantam, eh? I've drawn up some articles of agreement for you to look at"—all business, The Inimitable—"and I, sporting my True American, shall be an umpire known as the Gad's Hill Gasper. Fields and I have laid out the course—a mere six miles or so to Newton Center and back. It was covered with ice and snow, needless to say, when we did it. A most murderous way to cure a cough."

I wrote a letter home, prattling about "the superb energy" of the Chief, telling my family how "delighted" villainous Osgood and I were to provide him with this entertainment. Yes. Moving my thighs in public with ice about my ears because the Chief was bored. Our waiter smiled at me when he served the consommé that night, and I sneered into his red square Irish face "No potatoes, mind. And no familiarities." This pleased the Chief, though he whispered—his face burlesqued the cautious traveler—that we had to befriend the natives lest they eat us. Cannibal calling the cooking pot black.

But we all went laughing to the Mill Dam Road, and huddled over Osgood's silver brandy flask, shivering. The Chief was a snowman, all frozen brows, his mustache hung with tiny icicles. But he kept laughing. So we began, the ladies cheering—most of them, then, returning to the fire-lighted parlor as we left—and the Chief crabbed behind us, bellowing encouragements to Dolby, the mount he'd entered in the race. When you walk as quickly as you can, your hips swivel lewdly, and your breath fails at once, especially if, as I had, you'd spent so much of your time with tobacco and drink. I was gasping before the turn, and at the turning itself I saw before me little red and yellow shapes, such as you might watch in the medical college microscope. They stayed no matter how many times I blinked. Behind them it was all white, soon enough, and I hardly heard my wheezes. Not a sound from little Osgood, though, who smiled even then—he turned his head as he passed me—and slithered ahead. He wanted to win for the Chief, I had no doubt. And I was horrified to find that I did too, at least to shield myself from his generous humor, should I lose.

Mrs. Fields, the publisher's wife, was to await the winner at the finish-line, in the company of one or two other viciously pleased noncontestants, with a portion of bread soaked in brandy. Seeing that Osgood was ahead, she directed her carriage driven toward us—at this time, I was trying not to fall down, and welcomed the thought of a ride—but had it stopped behind Osgood's perky trail. Then she told the man to turn it, and drove alongside him; with silver serving tongs, she dropped a piece of brandy-soaked bread into his peeping birdlet's mouth. I stood where I was. I was overwhelmed by a need to urinate. The Chief in his carriage roared "On, Dolby!"

I replied "Sod, and go bugger!" But not with much volume. How often does food shout protests at the mouth it's lifted to? I walked to them, sauntered on my frozen feet, my hands in my pockets and my whiskers rimed so heavily my face felt dead—

I thought I was becoming like him. So I smiled, to crack the layering ice. He thought I smiled for him. Good dog.

I smiled too, but inside my skull, as I watched him sneeze throughout the dinner he gave in our honor in the Crystal Room of the Parker that night. I had thought he was dying, that he'd suffered a seizure in England and hadn't received right treatment for it (if treatment there was), and the reading tour thus far had confirmed my feelings. It was suicide for a man in his poor health to make the journey to America and then exhaust himself with such ferocious work. He said he did it for his children. I told myself he did it for the adulation which the groundlings gave him. But seeing him pale beneath the pallor of the ice which hung on him I thought that day, and later that night, of my original judgment: suicide. Why did he want so much to die? But he was a genius, I was not. He had written more of death, more movingly, than I would know in all my life.

Which didn't prevent me from smiling to my most appreciative self as he shivered and sneezed and coughed even harder in the grips of an oncoming illness he'd beseeched in order to see me jump on his strings. His spirits were high, though, and he drank a good deal, joking with Lowell and Holmes, Norton, Longfellow and his daughter, others of like reputation and dignified Bostonian bearing. I think he puzzled them. His running nose and yellow eyes were entertainment, though, for me—despite my concern that he'd pushed his health beyond its reserves.

At about ten, Osgood and the Chief and I went up to bed. His bath had been drawn, and he insisted on our presence as he undressed for the tub. His left leg was swollen and the area around the toes was puffy. When he saw my attention to it, he limped exaggeratedly to the tub's edge, sat on it, and began to whistle and smile, saying "Grimaldi at the ocean's edge, eh, Dolby?"

Osgood smiled his gums and nodded, though he'd never seen the actor—nor had I, though I knew his reputation—and I said "It's an ocean you could drink, sir."

"Ho!" he called, teetering. "Ha!" In his evening coat and boutonniere, trouserless and swelling, he rolled and whistled, clowning as I'd seen him do for whatever audience he could muster, usually his ten delighted children and his silent smiling wife. "A-*hey!*" he called, wobbling, thrusting his arms forward, losing his balance no matter, and falling into the tub—coat and golden chains and the carapace of brilliantined hair.

I said "On, sir!" as I went to help him out.

On the train, next day, he wrote a letter in shaking hand which I was to manage to get delivered to New York in time for a Cunard sailing. He complained of his quakings and cough, saying that "My True American has taken a fresh start, and I have terrified poor Dolby quite out of his wits by setting in for a paroxysm of sneezing." The letter was urgent, he said, because it contained a command to his eldest daughter that one Holman be asked for an estimate "1. To recover, with red leather, all the dining room chairs. 2. To ditto, with green leather, all the library chairs and the couch."

I said "The postal connection will be difficult to make, sir."

Looking out the window, he said "The recovering, Dolby, is of the utmost importance to me. I have taken it into my head to have it done, and I will have it done. A house needs renewing."

Your humble servant.

So on, then, to Syracuse, Rochester, Buffalo, and then Albany again, carrying the light of the world by train.

He grew worse. His True American seemed to hinder his breathing at times, and I often had to read out signs for him. At Syracuse, he had great difficulty in walking: he called it "an eruption of the leg." But he talked incessantly, of the recovering, with lovely malice of the pirating of his books by American publishers, and of the food, which, though he ate so little, was of great importance to him: "Old buffalo for breakfast again, I see."

And he grew worse. Syracuse was a great success, of course, and some boys who had ridden miles from a small college called Hamilton wrote in their newspaper an article, reprinted in the local press, which was a hymn to his greatness. The Chief was enraged. "Read this, Dolby! They have no education at that place. They're training valets. *Grooms!*" It said "How did he look? Well, he *was* dressed a wee bit foppish, for so snowy a mustache, but after all with faultless taste. His great Shakespearean collar was very neat and white, so was his white tie, so was his white bosom. And the three little gold studs on his breast fairly laughed—" He became silenter and more depressed, saying he would not be accused by tadpoles of being *nouveau riche*.

The newspapers in the area—a more backward place than the westernmost frontiers, he said—endlessly speculated about him— that he had recently sent five thousand dollars to his sister-in-law (with the implication that such a transaction meant a relationship barely moral, probably illegal); that he had asked the Secretary of the Treasury not to make assessment of the proceeds of his readings; that he would come to such-and-such a village to read its charter aloud, if they would pay him sufficiently—and the more said about his private life, the paler, more morose, he became. When we received a cable about the death of his friend Chauncey Townshend, he told me "Everyone is starting to die, now. When that happens, Dolby, there is an astringent stinking of mortality over everything, like a foul cloud."

Then something called "the freshet" happened. Between Rochester and Albany, we were caught by storms and the power of late March sunlight. A river named the Mohawk rose with water and ice, and the river became blocked. Driftwood and enormous chunks of dirty gray ice flooded onto the tracks sometimes to a depth of several feet, the tracks were impassable, rails were lifted off. We couldn't go on, we had to stay at Utica.

He fairly shook with fury in his lounge seat when the train stopped, hissing, at a darkened terminal. "I don't *want* to sleep in places named Utica" he said. "I want to go home."

He had learned from the motorman that Secretary of State Seward was stranded with him, though Seward was in a private car which was pulled at the end of the train. "You don't suppose he reads novels, do you? If their President interviewed with me—though he barely said a word that qualified him for low office, much less high—perhaps their Secretary of State, who is *not* being impeached, might consider—"

"Yes, sir?"

"An overnight guest?"

"No, sir."

"Why *no*, Dolby?" His eyes were narrowed, his nostrils wide. Although he wore a decent brown suit and his little round top hat and his gold waist chains, he looked like one of his murderers, bereft of hope, immersed in death, fearfully enjoying his victim's fear, and his own. "Pray, inform me why you wish to see me wrapped in a stale coverlet at some stale home for orphaned fleas in this stalest of gray-green cities."

"Politicians in America don't read words, sir. They only speak them. And read only numbers. You've written of it yourself."

"Twenty-five years ago, Dolby. Now, I'm not what you might call inconsequential, am I?"

"To politicians, sir, you are."

"Damn you."

"Yes, sir."

"Damn them *all!*"

So he limped to a wooden bench near a baggage camion, comforted by servile Osgood, and sat in a pool of dim light, his legs stretched before him: an inconsolable boy. I walked near a street named Genesee, as I'd been directed, and in the city's other hotel, called Baggs', I requested rooms. The clerk was very thin and breathed through his mouth as he bent, his nose almost touching the page of the register, to examine our names. "Him" he said. "I heard of him. I'n't he English?"

A little cannon gave its cough near the train, and I said "That's he they're saluting now, I suspect."

"Nope." His breath should have been the color of Stilton. "Seward." I knew who else would make the same mistake, and be similarly corrected, and I smiled.

At the station again, Osgood stood when I approached and nodded his head at the large boy on the bench. The Chief looked up from the railroad guide and said "I'm really most entertained, Dolby. I know now that one can travel from here to famous Deansville in twenty minutes. And that the Franklin run is eight minutes less. Indeed. And that Mister John Butterfield is the superintendent of these runs, and it's he we've to thank for ordering the trains shut down. How can I properly give voice to my appreciation of this diversion?"

Then he said nothing more as I and Osgood—he was silent, and always, now, enraged—carried the bags (porters, it seems had been swept away by the freshet) up four dark streets past wooden buildings and one or two monuments to the last century, and entered Baggs' four-story brick hotel, with its papered walls and imitation-English hunting prints, and two huge clocks, each of which kept its own time. We shared a suite, the Chief in the bedroom, Osgood and I on sofa and cot in the sitting room. In about half an hour, Moses Baggs came calling with sandwiches and wine, and his ample hates.

The Chief greeted him with the usual charm he reserved for close friends and important businessmen and politicians: head erect, left hand in trousers pocket, chest swelled to set off his waistcoat chains which draped him, a primrose and black dressing gown opened all the way; his mouth curved down, his nostrils were wide, his eyes were hooded. He didn't smile, but made gentle motions in the air with his hands, as if to say how much at peace he was, now that Baggs had come. Some of that tranquillity was the deadness of his left cheek and jaw: linen stretched taut.

They sat across an oval carved table from one another, drinking to each other, neither eating, probably so as not to lose the sense of utter sufficiency each one tried to radiate. Baggs was stockier than the Chief, dressed more quietly in broadcloth and a bow tie, bat-wing collar. His lips curved downward too, but they were more compressed, suggesting resistance and disapproval at once. His nose was broad and hooked, quite gracefully, and his eyes, in large sockets, looked small. He was as vain about his straight silky hair as the Chief was vain about his much-pomaded curls, and he combed it across his forehead as a youngster in school might do.

They spoke without humor and, although Osgood and I were near the sitting room fireplace, across the room from the adjoining door, and could hear only murmurs and sometimes the fragments of words, we watched while sitting opposite one another's wing chairs to see how the rural landlord received the man who'd made a nation weep.

Osgood leaned over, as if to prod a burning log with the brass poker, and whispered "He looks like a country parson."

"He's talking to the high priest."

Osgood nodded his small head, his fine tight features. "The grand vizier. High poop and God-almighty godling."

"Don't be bitter, Osgood. He's given you a chance."

"Sure. At a smaller salary. And the loss of my job when he squeals to Fields. I run his errands like a cabin boy and never get thanked."

"Osgood: you *cheated*."

"I used my imagination to better myself. Just like him. He came from nothing too, though he'd never admit it."

"He admits it all the time. The trouble, I'm afraid, is that you aren't bright enough to perceive it. That's why you cheated so clumsily, and got caught. And after what your machinations put me through, you won't get sympathy from me, my friend. Or any conversational betrayals. That one is a great man."

Osgood crossed his little legs without wrinkling his trousers, rubbed his small fingers across his still clean-shaven jaws, sighed loudly, and shook his head. "No, sir, Dolby. No. It doesn't work. I'm not convinced. No doubt I'm stupider than you. You're fooling him in ways that don't get caught, sure. But you're cheating nevertheless, and you can't say no. I've seen you read his mail, for instance, haven't I?"

"Witling! He gives me his letters to post. I have to address and seal them. *That's* what you've seen."

"Oh."

"Don't oh me. Don't be smug with your betters, friend."

"Ah, *friend*. And you watch him all the time. Look at him like he's chicken on your plate. You're doing something crooked, Dolby. Our little lamb shouldn't trust you very far."

"Osgood. I'm tired, and my p-patience is thin as my hair."

"Very g-good, Mister Dolby."

"B-buggering imp!"

"Your servant, M-mister Dolby."

I was considering how best to bash him with the fire iron when the Chief raised his voice—that splendid baritone he used for summoning ghosts from the back of his mind to the stage—and called "Dolby! Can you join us a moment?"

I went in, half bowing, to say "Mister Baggs? Sir?"

"We've had a curious conversation, Dolby. I thought I'd put you in the way of it, since we share so much." Which meant that I was now a foil. Costumed character. A theatrical event. "I cautiously inquired of Mr. Baggs, our host, as to the disposition of fire steps. America's the land of hotel fires, I said, and I am, as you know, disinclined to be roasted in foreign flames."

"Yes, sir. We've seen our share of smoke the past months."

"Yes, we have. So I tendered my inquiry"—he nodded to Baggs and smiled his unfelt smile— "only to learn that our host is unsympathetic to suggestions that flammability, a universal law, extends to his historical pile."

In a hard high voice Baggs said, to the table, "My hotel, which is built where my father's inn stood safely for more years than you can count, is the safest hotel in the Mohawk Valley."

"In the entire Mohawk Valley, Dolby!"

Baggs said "Brick throughout, and the most seasoned wood."

The Chief pounced like a ratcatcher: "Definition of an oven, I should say, eh, Dolby? No matter, though. We're safe in your hands. Taken as read. *You*, then, to return to the narrative, said—correct me, please, if I misrepresent you—'I understand that you work in the way of prostitutes.' Am I correct, sir?"

"You surely understand," Baggs said, "that I spoke of reformed prostitutes. Women of the streets now turned to women of virtue by virtue of yourself and some rich woman over there who shares your, ah, interest."

"Dedication, sir, not interest. I have no *interest* in whores. I work toward the cleansing of society by helping to remove them from the hovels and thoroughfares. Once the pollution's contained, and they're lodged in a well-regulated home under watchful eyes, I contribute a small amount of money, and a large amount of my time, and address them once a year to remind them of the holiness in which they must again learn to hold themselves."

"Very generous" Baggs said.

"And that 'rich woman' of whom you speak derisively is Mrs. Coutts, whose generosity and dedication are unsurpassed."

"Except by your own" Baggs said. "You are known for your generosity to women, may I say."

"No." The Chief's nose was whiter than his pale face, and his eyes were Jonas Chuzzlewitt's, squatting over a warm corpse. "No. Do not. There's an inference in what you say."

"Inferences are as taken" Baggs said, folding his arms across his chest, almost smiling. "I'm enjoying our talk."

"You must have enjoyed your Civil War as well."

"No, killing's not *my* line of work."

"Dolby! My God! Am I hearing this? *Mister* Baggs: I have worked long hours to the ends of my strength and ingenuity in order to make our lives more happy. Hundreds of thousands of people, each month—every *day*—have—"

"Made you rich. I'm pleased for you."

The Chief stood, then sat as if his leg had given out. His face pulsed red and hot, then paler. He stood again, gold chains clanking, to stare down into Baggs' arrogant eyes, and whispered "You may not know who I am, although you know my name. You may not know *what* I am, although your most tobacco-sodden countrymen have acquainted themselves with that intelligence. I am here to read from my works, and you may pay to hear me do so if the revenue derived from this Mohawk Valley pleasure-dome permits such an outlay. But you may no longer hear my words for nothing."

"All right" Baggs said, standing, "I don't believe it's worth the price, and will have to deny myself any more noise like this. *You* may pay in the morning, at the downstairs desk. Thank you for your custom. And be damned." He left at an even easy pace, clicking the door gently closed.

The Chief sent me away, and through the closed door, whenever

I wakened on the horsehair sofa, I saw the light beneath his door.
I had no doubt he was writing it, transmogrifying it, for someone,
but there was no letter in the morning, and the letter he gave me
two days later said "The train gave in altogether at Utica, and the
passengers were let loose there for the night. As I was due at Al-
bany, a very active superintendent of works did all he could to get
us along, and in the morning we resumed our journey through the
water, with a hundred men in seven-league boots pushing the ice
from before us with long poles." Eaten for supper in Utica!

Our train was moist and hot, Osgood was sullen, the Chief in
much pain. He sat panting near a window open to the long fields
and flooded railroad bed, he said nothing. Four men walked before
the train, pushing the ice aside, and children at the rails called
to us not to hurry, and to ride a horse. Our train took on the passen-
gers of two other trains on which the fires had been put out by
high water twenty-four hours before; so the seats were all filled,
the air too muggy for comfortable breathing, and what there was
of it was rank with the body sweat of farmers and the less ex-
cusably unwashed. The Chief held a newspaper in front of his head
and leaned his face at the window so as to be unnoticed. Everyone
stared at the man whose shoulders ended in paper and ink.

At the second transfer of passengers, we watched as cattle and
sheep were unloaded from the train alongside. A dozen of the sheep
were dead—our motorman explained they get maggots by the dozen
as soon as they're cut, so septic is their wool—because they'd been
stranded so long without feed that in their hunger they had begun
to eat one another. The Chief's eyes widened and their fire jumped.
He couldn't look away from the corpses of sheep, and the ones
that staggered with bleeding wounds. "Horrible, Dolby. Ghastly to
look at. Look!" He stared through the window and wrinkled his
nose in disgust. He stared, said "Wond'rous sights in the New
World. Most horrible, my God. Never, never—"

Osgood said "Sure."

So we reached Albany, cutting through ice, with spring in the air
outside, foulness within, and then a sudden change, more snow. I
wondered if he would live through the reading, and then the trips
to Boston and New York, then home. I think he wondered too. And
I'm sure that Osgood prayed for a timely seizure, a week of mourn-
ing, his freedom. I prayed for myself.

The Chief drank iced brandy and water in a weak solution, then dragged his foot to the front of the stage in a swarm of applause. By the time he was half a dozen feet from the lectern, his walk was balanced and steady as that of a great man's butler. At a side door, below the boxes, I watched his hatred for his body, and his love for the people's love—he thought that he loved *them*—transformed to a combination of scorn, for both himself and them, and a sly greengrocer's gratitude: Mrs. Gamp, in the most slum-dusted Cockney, said, from the hairy hurt mouth of a man for whom little laughter was left, " 'A thing,' she said, 'as hardly ever, Mrs. Mould, occurs with me unless it is when I am indisposed, and find my pint of porter settling heavy on the chest. Mrs. Harris often and often says to me, "Sairey Gamp," she says, "you raly do amaze me!" ' "

Then—I had seen his specially printed prompt copies, with their crossings-out, revisions, and their stage directions in the margin, *Breathe deeply here*, or *Horror! Disbelief!*, in red ink—he was soon to Mrs. Prig's perfidy, as Gamp's best friend Mrs. Harris, so often quoted, is revealed as only her febrile imagination, a ghost in her waking dreams. "Mrs. Gamp resumed: 'Mrs. Harris, Betsey—'

" 'Bother Mrs. Harris!' said Mrs. Prig.

"Mrs. Gamp looked at her with amazement, incredulity, and indignation; when Mrs. Prig, shutting her eye still closer, and folding her arms still tighter, uttered these memorable and tremendous words: 'I don't believe there's no sich a person!'

"The shock of this blow was so violent and sudden, that Mrs. Gamp sat staring at nothing with uplifted eyes, and her mouth open as if she were gasping for breath."

Etc. Yrs Sincerely, etc.

Dressed in what they assumed the English, whom they said they scorned, might wear to an evening's theater, they pointed and laughed—to hear the London diction, and to ridicule it; to share with the Chief his derision of the lower classes (whom he said he shielded from upper-class snobbery) and to thus be aligned with the landed and rich, whom their native comics daily wreaked their parodies on; to punish the audacities of imagination, though it was not just their evening's meal, but the chef who roasted *them*.

I saw, in the gas light hissing above him, that his right jaw clenched and unclenched like the beating breast of a bird. He stood with his weight on his right leg, and his hands shook. The spectators doubtless laid it to his emotional raptures, perhaps even the subject matter which followed—Little Dombey's nauseous dying —but I knew that his final energies were giving out. Osgood, at his post across the hall from me, stood with his hands in his pockets and probably thought of how to convince old Fields that he was pure. I wondered how to convince old Dolby that *I* was.

"The golden ripple on the wall came back again, and nothing else stirred in the room." He was whispering, and the weeping from the orchestra seats seemed to feed his clever grief. "The old, old fashion! The fashion that came in with our first garments, and will last unchanged until our race has run its course, and the wide firmament is rolled up like a scroll. The old, old fashion,—Death!

"O, thank God, all who see it, for that older fashion yet, of Immortality! And look upon us, Angels of young children, with regards not quite estranged, when the swift river bears us to the ocean!"

Pause at Estranged. Lingering sigh.

And then backstage: a greater exhaustion than usual. I was certain America would see the Chief give in to apoplexy and an attack of paralysis. His muscles jumped under his clothes, and his voice was husky, harsh. The Murder was next, and he held the prompt copy on his old man's lap. I said nothing of his first part's success, or of his fading strength. Instead, I squatted before him (wagging my tail) and said "Sir, the schedule you have given me for our next readings has something in common with this. Can you guess it?"

"No games now, Dolby. I'm spent."

"Out of four readings, sir, you have put down three Murders."

"And?"

"And since the success of the tour is so thoroughly assured, and since it no longer makes a jot of difference what you read, perhaps you will refrain from savaging your constitution every evening. You suffer most horribly after a Murder . . ."

"Have you finished?"

"As you want it."

"I've said all I will say on the matter!" He threw a knife and fork to the backstage floor; his plate—the food untouched—fell too, and was smashed. "Dolby! Your infernal caution will be your ruin one of these days!"

"Perhaps, sir. But in this case, I hope you will recall that it was exercised in your interest."

Yrs etc., G. Dolby.

Then back to the applause, the darkness of the hall, the fearful women in the audience who had read in their papers of the fainting women in other halls, the men who prepared—their handkerchiefs were folded on their knees—to weep as their countrymen had done in other cities for many months.

When I returned to my post, Osgood was there, wearing his bulky cloak and shod for snow. I said "Are you chilly?"

"I'm going" he whispered. "I won't be used like this."

"Won't you? And like what?"

"Handmaiden to that great girl up there in front of his violet screen and his hand-tuned gas lamp. Not any more. He can have me sacked, and roast in hell's own fire for his troubles. I don't care. *I'll* be my own man, Dolby."

"Meaning what, you sack of shit?"

"Meaning he owns these geese sitting here so dutifully. He owns you to your shoes. And he'd like to own me. The whole *world*. This is a free country, no one'll have me that way. No, sir. And he'll burn. He'll burn."

I yawned as hard as I could and whispered "Goodnight, Osgood. Do write us for references, won't you?"

"Not where he'll be writing 'em from, Mister D-Dolby."

I felt him leave. My tongue was locked on my teeth. I closed my eyes and listened as Nancy, in the Chief's near-falsetto—true enough to be a frightened woman's tremulous croon—said to the monster she wholly loved " 'Why do you look like that at me!'

"The robber sat regarding her for a few seconds with dilated nostrils and heaving breast, and then, grasping her by the head and throat, dragged her into the middle of the room, and looking once towards the door, placed his heavy hand upon her mouth."

Now: despair.

" 'Bill, Bill!' gasped the girl, wrestling with the strength of mortal fear—'I—I won't scream or cry—not once—hear me—speak to me—tell me what I have done!' "

A woman in the rear, knowing she was supposed to, wept.

" 'You know, you she-devil!' returned the robber, suppressing his breath. 'You were watched tonight; every word you said was heard.' "

It still held me in its fist and shook me—not so much the fear but the lust to kill, the terrible passion for death he summoned into the dark air. And, I admit it, the destruction it worked on his feeble body by the end. I opened my eyes, more people were quaking with tears. His eyes were bright as fresh coals, and he loved his hatred, his face against the background screen was that of a corpse. And then I saw that above his head, protruding from the stalls, the gas light reflector on its copper wire was threatened by a carelessly placed gas jet. Its flame was high, it was heating the wires. Once burned through, they would release the reflector, which would fall into the stalls and set the theater afire.

Which of us had failed to oversee the gas man place his lamp? Or: which of us—the thought came smoothly into place—had over-seen him most zealously. Had moved the lamp ourselves, perhaps, with the tremble of a hand snaked down from the stalls when the theater was empty. Which of us had settled on a damp hall in Albany, State of New York, for suicide bier? And which of us had sought not suicide, but murder?

The wires glowed red, and I watched them. They grew larger, he diminished, and his voice sank away from my ears. The wires pulsed, and I studied them. He would burn first if the reflector fell, and his vision of flame would be true. His visions so often were. I stayed at my place. " 'You *shall* have time to think, and save yourself this crime; I will not loose my hold, you cannot throw me off. For dear God's sake, for your own, for mine, stop before you spill my blood!' "

I pushed at the door, which led to the carpeted corridor, out to a cobbled alley, away. I let it press back against my hand. Something made me—makes me—shake my head. I walked on my toes to the backstage steps and on my hands and knees (how right had Osgood been?) I crept behind the violet screen and, where its corner protruded behind the folded stage curtain, watched from my squat. He bounced on his toes, his hands moved in health through the air. He was pawing his prey.

I hissed. His eyes struck down and sideways, and I stared up into them, and stared. Then I looked up at the cooking wires, pointed, opened my mouth as if to cry aloud, whispered "How long?"

The murderer's eyes lay on me like shovels-ful of wet earth. He didn't look up, but straight ahead, at his audience—at Nancy, begging for life—and then he let them fall on me again, studying.

One murderer's eye slowly closed into a rogue's long wink. He showed two fingers behind the podium, then closed his hand in a fist. He had seen it all, perhaps before I had. He was relishing his courage, timing himself to finish before the flaming fall. I crawled back and sat on the floor, my head against the cold brick wall. I closed my eyes and rolled my head from side to side, thinking of Osgood. I knew he was thinking of us.

The Chief skipped parts, improvising elision and connection with invisible seams. I improvised too, for I was certain he would ask why I'd waited so long before warning him. And I was only Dolby, the clever character who did his bidding. I had no powers of my own for invention. I had no powers then for even simple thought. I was as limp as a dropped doll. Wood and paste don't answer.

Nancy was saying " 'Bill, Bill, for dear God's sake, for your own, for mine, stop before you spill my blood! I have been true to you, upon my guilty soul I have!' "

I heard his teeth click, and the spit pop from his mouth into the hot bright air around him. I knew that his eyes were bulging, his head shaking as if he froze, that the audience was stiff with expectation and emotion, that the wires were burning and the fire he feared, was always expecting, nodded above him as if in answer to what he constantly asked. The doxy and plunderer wailed to one another, pulling at each other, by his language bound.

" 'Bill,' cried the girl, striving to lay her head upon his breast, 'the gentleman and that dear lady told me tonight of a home in some foreign country where I could end my days in solitude and peace. Let me see them again, and beg them, on my knees, to show the same mercy and goodness to you; and let us both leave this dreadful place, and far apart lead better lives, and forget how we have lived, except in prayers, and never see each other more. It is never too late to repent. They told me so—I feel it now—but we must have time—a little, little time!' "

There was a rustle, and I knew that someone led a fainting woman from her seat. *Faster here. Profundo.*

"The housebreaker freed one arm and grasped his pistol. The certainty of immediate detection if he fired, flashed across his mind even in the midst of his fury; and he beat it twice with all the force he could summon, upon the upturned face that almost touched his own."

Screams and whimpers from the seats.

Remorseless, unrelenting.

"She staggered and fell, nearly blinded with the blood that rained down from a deep gash in her forehead, but raising herself, with difficulty, on her knees, drew from her bosom a white handkerchief—pure Rose Maylie's own— "*Innocence! Vaguest hope!—*" and sighed 'No, Bill! NO!' Then, weaker, holding the handkerchief up, in her folded hands, as high towards Heaven as her feeble strength would allow, she breathed in prayer for mercy to her Maker.

"It was a ghastly figure to look upon." *Slow down here.* "The murderer, staggering backward to the wall and shutting out the sight with his hand, seized a heavy club and struck her down."

First the shell of silence, then the bellows and cries of *Bravo!* which cracked the shell. The clapping of hands: a ceremony of drums. And in its midst, his growling "Gas down, there! Turn it off! Turn off the *gas*, you imbecile!"

And finally, then, the fire-lit bedroom of his suite, where he lay in the bed, a coverlet on his still-shod feet, breathing wheezily, slowly, untouched food and champagne on the bedside table. His eyes were closed, his left hand curled in a child's sleeping clench. As I watched, tears ran slowly onto his white-yellow cheeks. He still lived the killing. He might have wept for being killed, for doing the murder, for both.

In a very small voice he said "We gave them more than their money's worth, Dolby."

"You were magnificent, sir. I still, after all these Murders, am shaken by it."

"Yes. Osgood is gone?"

"Thieves in the night, and so on."

"He arranged the gas jet?"

"No, I don't think so. No: I mean I'm not sure. He never seemed to have the imagination or nerve."

"I've driven lesser men to do more, Dolby. It *might* have been he. I'll write to Fielding in the morning, anyway. See you post it before we leave."

"Yes, sir." I looked into the fire, then saw that he looked there too, the tears still on his face. "We are booked on the *Russia*, sir, a Cunarder of course. From New York, as you directed, to Liverpool. To arrive the 22nd of April, and I, for one, will be delighted."

"We cannot help but be transported, Dolby. Yes, I'll kiss the docks when we disembark, I promise it. Home is where you go to die. Not hothouse hotels in cities with pretentious names."

"Not you, sir. Some rest, perhaps a start on a new—"

"Dolby, please don't interfere in my schedule of writing. That is my concern, and bookings and arrangements are yours. Oh, Dolby, damn all, I apologize. And for snapping—before, about the Murder. I'm too tired, aren't I?"

He looked into the fire—partly because he was embarrassed, I think. He rarely apologized, except to the likes of Collins, say, or maybe still Forster, and hardly even to them.

I said "A late squall of snow is expected tomorrow, I'm told. I wonder if you would consider staying in at the fireside and resting?"

He lay as if he had no muscles, said "Was there an afternoon post?"

"No letters from England, sir."

"No. I wonder how the children are, and everyone, that's all."

"I'm sure you're in mind at home as strongly as if you were there."

Pause here.

"Are you sorry, Dolby, for all the woe and work I've put you to?" The scoundrel. "No, sir. I've—"

"Served. Miraculously."

"I was going to say I've learned."

His head turned toward the fire, his arms and legs lay loose. He sighed, as if half into sleep, "Learned what, my good, good Dolby?"

"You cannot imagine, sir."

Breathless silence.

I backed towards the door.

Deeper silence, still.

I saw the red pen moving in the margins, smoke of his language poured up. I booked his halls and blacked his boots. I was his page. He made me what I am.

New strength. A wicked low laugh.

"Can't I, Dolby?" *Dolby leans against door. Perspiration. In the darkness, pain.* "Haven't I?"

THE CHICAGO POEM

JEROME ROTHENBERG

for Ted Berrigan & Alice Notley

the bridges of Chicago
are not the bridges of Paris
or the bridges of Amsterdam
except they are a definition
almost no one bothers to define
like life full of surprises
in what now looks to be the oldest
modern American city
o apparition of the movie version of
the future circa 1931
the bridges soon filled with moving lines
of people workers' armies
in the darkness of first December visit
along the water
bend of the Chicago River
the cliffs of architecture like palisades
at night the stars in windows
stars in the poem you wrote a sky
through which the el train pulls its lights
in New York streets of childhood
is like a necklace (necktie) in the language of
old poems old memories

old Fritz Lang visions of the night before
the revolution the poor souls
of working people we all love
fathers or uncles
lost to us in dreams & gauze
of intervening 1960s
there are whole tribes of Indians
somewhere inhabiting
a tunnel paradise
they will wait it out still
with a perfect assurance of things to come
everyone so well read in old novels
maybe the economics of disaster Ted
depressions of the spirit
so unlike the bright promise of
the early years
gloss of the young life easing death
atop a hill in Lawrence Kansas
the afternoon sky became aluminum
(illumination)
played on a tambourine to calm
the serpent fear
the material corpse that leaves us vulnerable
everyone will come to it I think
I do not think you dig it
getting so out of hand so far away
but we remain & I will
make another visit soon
hope we can take a walk
together it is night & we are
not so bad off have turned forty
like poets happy with our sadness
we are still humans in a city overhung
with ancient bridges
you pop your pill I laugh
look back upon the future of
America & remember
when we both wrote our famous poems called
Modern Times

THE MOON, THE OWL, MY SISTER

COLEMAN DOWELL

We are an agrarian family, living by the field. We have been taught that those who live by the field will die by the field, and we accept this. We are necessarily nomadic. Our belief in the equal division of landed property is not shared by the owners of the property we till and work, and thus we must move on from field to field, gleaning as much of the harvest as we can, using the residue of its materials to build our seasonal homes. Sometimes we fall onto good seasons, a double-edged remark, for by it I mean those times when land is allowed to lie fallow, and we must then go far afield for our food; but, the good edge, in such seasons we put down roots and foolishly, according to our mother, build dwellings that have about them the look and feel of permanence.

For the past two hunter's moons we have lived in one of these "permanent" dwellings. We add on rooms as the fancy strikes, and fill storehouses as though we at last had come into property of our very own, which no one could take from us by revolution or otherwise. "Otherwise" must remain undefined, for it is the stuff of instinct; but "revolution," as we define it, would grant us the right to our piece of earth, which would be no larger or smaller than those of our fellows, and so covetousness could not have a part to play.

We are a small family though we have in the past been large.

Indeed, the lady of the house whom I gratefully call mother is in fact my stepmother, and in this sense "our family" is a comparatively recent term. My own mother, the product of whose loins by my father I am the remaining specimen, was taken from us when I was very small, though I remember her well. My father formed the new alliance as much for my sake as for his own, and the excellent creature he took to spouse has provided him with another brood, diminished now. Altogether we are only six; two of us were taken in hunting accidents, one by drowning, and another is simply gone, we know not where.

My favorite sister—though the word looks unfair, as I have only one other now, a baby still—is beautiful, poetic, and moody, and was born to my stepmother in her first alliance, before I was conceived.

Our father is stalwart and revered, and though sometimes we laugh at him, it is my belief that he deliberately fosters it to relieve rebellious instincts. We seldom quarrel among ourselves, due to the peaceable example of our parents, and we are allowed a large degree of independence meant to develop our individuality. That some of us have died is thankfully not seen as the result of such latitude, and we are not made to suffer in addition to our sense of loss.

In our current situation—may it continue unbroken and unresolved, which supplication I will try to make clear in the course of this narrative—we each have our own rooms, which reflect our independence nicely. My youngest brother and sister, whom we refer to as "the twins" though they are the survivors of sextuplets, have made their connecting quarters into one labyrinth, diabolically intricate; to visit them one must be prepared to stay awhile.

My room, because of my "thoughtful" bent, is plainest, and though I do not have any books entire, I have sections of books which I have arranged as I have seen them in houses (the houses from which I took the leaves, patiently unlawful, a leaf at a time); among these are almost all of the f's and m's from a dictionary (Microtus pennsylvanicus rather proudly underlined); there is also a shattering poem by Robert Burns and, a dark and perhaps sinful secret, parts of many adventures from a curious book called *Master Tyll Owlglass*.

My favorite sister's room is the one we are most eager to be invited to visit, for it is both strange and cozy. She has allowed—

proof of that good housekeeper, our mother's benevolence!—cob-
webs to accumulate, entire with occupants and sometimes their
would-be dinners. In most cases both occupant and prey are pre-
served in the mere likeness of life, but there is always at least one
active web and one can sit before it and watch the tragicomedy of
life and death and meditate upon it, as my sister frequently
does. My mother, somewhat testily, is accustomed to say that this
spectacle accounts for a certain streak of morbidity in my beloved
sister. But as to my view of it, I will only say, not wishing to dis-
pute our mother more than necessary, that the word—morbidity—
seems at odds with my sister. As I have said, she is poetical, which
means, I believe, that she is more prone to meditations upon fate
than others among us, but within herself I believe the word would
not find a congenial atmosphere. Unless morbid and philosophical
are synonyms bound together, like halves of a peach pit, by a
seamlike thread that we can acknowledge to be poetical foresight.

And yet. The owl in winter flying low and calling draws her,
draws her like a thread from the upper world. Draws her out of
her room and toward the door. The look on her face at such times
is one a brother would like to erase, or to forget. And yet it is
not morbid, or has not seemed so since my dreams began. For the
moment I will characterize the look thusly: it is intent, as though
she hears a music in the cry that we cannot; it is curious, as though
words were being used that she does not, but would, understand;
and it is something other. My mother and I, the watchers,
would have that "something" changed for another look, one that
remembered us, for at such times we are forgotten. She will walk
among us as we are gathered together for warmth and pleasure,
and will not see us, the multiple expression upon her rapt coun-
tenance creating the face of a stranger. Even now, with the insight
I have obtained through dreams, I find it disquieting to dwell at
length upon that look, that unfamiliar face.

Curiously, my father does not seem to share the apprehension
that my mother and I feel. When my sister sleepwalks through our
little group, father will loudly say something about the quality of
the corn we are eating, and perhaps even toss a grain at my sis-
ter's head, but if he does it to bring her out of her trance, one has
the feeling that it is done without awareness or planning. His pro-
tectiveness toward us extends the length of him, like a backbone.

We all hear the owl. Some of us tremble to hear it cry its shivery

cry so close to our lock, but this lack of control is confined to the
dead of winter when the frost has pushed the entranceway to our
house moonward. And though the tremblers may be soothed by
our mother's quiet caress, the reason is never spoken of. We learned
the name of the author of such a fearsome song in the fields, among
our playmates. Because of the secrecy surrounding the name we
have come to know that to speak it before our parents would be to
mouth an obscenity, worse than to say "cheese" in polite society. We
spare our parents our knowledge of the name as they spare us; it is
for this reason that I keep *Master Tyll Owlglass* hidden, for I think
it would profoundly shock my mother. Nor do we children compare
notes among ourselves, such as "Did you hear the wings brush the
roof last night?" I think we all imagine something dire would follow
such confidence, and when we hear it each of our embarrassed
ruses to cover the sound could be considered comical.

My sister does not always make these spectral appearances
among us when the owl hunts. Many is the time she has sat with
us, and heard the swoop and the enticing cries, and only trembled.
Lately, since my revelation, once again she sits among us, but
without trembling, for it is as though she has divined that she has
an ally now, and need not—But I am unable to finish the thought.
A lot is clear to me that once was cloudy, but there are many
things that I would conclude, or draw conclusions about, that are
still veiled, and so I, like my sister, wait.

I would not give the impression that we live perpetually under
that shadow. If death, personified by the owl, inhabits the sky, so
does life in the presence of the sun. It is the sun that makes the
grain grow; it is the plenitude or lack of grain that most informs
our lives. And we are shortsighted.

Even the lesson of the cheese is taken as a laughing matter by
the twins, and during those exercises I confess that my mind wan-
ders. There is something ludicrous about that piece of rock-hard
cheese upon which we are instructed to concentrate our loathing. It
would scarcely seem to be the stuff that wistful dreams are made
on. My sister sits embarrassed during the lesson, for it was she who
was glancingly wounded; she wears her slight limp as penance
and to my mind, it is reminder enough. But twice a week the bait is
hauled out and we must howl our derision, hold our noses as
though it smelled to heaven.

The twins love the exercise for at those times they are allowed to chant and howl out the word that at other times can only be whispered behind the backs of our elders. Once I asked our mother if she did not think my sister took this somehow personally, as though she were the object of our concerted hatred, but mother assured me that it was standard procedure in the best households, even those that could not boast a survivor of the trap.

We are a happy family. Believe me, we are. The twins scamper outrageously, our parents teach us old games and invent new ones, my bookishness is the cause of both pride and amusement, for I have lied about how the library was acquired, and my sister, an artist, gives our household stature. Throughout the field we are known because of her. It is my belief that because of her, when last we had to move our dwelling, others chose to cluster around us, so that we are—a rarity among our breed—a community with a center and activities outside the home. Through the end of the season of goldenrod we played at our communal games; into the first frost we foraged as a community, sharing the spoils, as befits agrarians. Thus every storehouse is equally provisioned, except in the cases of overwhelmingly large families, who are given more. Nobody grumbles about this.

Now that winter approaches, we seldom visit back and forth, and in our house my sister's room is the scene, though by invitation only! of memorable evenings.

More of my sister's room: branches of berries against the cobwebs, pods of milkweed like hoary heads, a carpet of silvery husks. It is a fantasy room in which one, rustling, becomes part of the fantasy, as though one moved in an autumn field, dodging the moon, instead of in the safety and glamour of my sister's ambiance —a rare combination expressing my sister exactly where others are concerned; if there is no safety for *her* within that radiance beyond which we cannot reach, there is also little if any sense of personal glamour. In my sister's room there is no evidence of vanity, hardly anything of personal adornment. To amuse us, she may wear a wig of corn silk, or, playing a great lady, a necklace of strung bittersweet, but she is at her best when she parodies the ways of the world without props or costumes, stretching our imaginations through her pantomime.

Her purest success is chrysalis-into-butterfly. She always stops in her dance with the maiden flight of the enchanted insect, at the peak of its intoxicated freedom, and the tragedy of its brief hour is tacit. For the youngest among us, it is unimaginable, for the twins are blessed with immortality, conviction being the soul of philosophy. That the flight of the butterfly is in the direction of one of the webs, that a "wing" brushes a web, is the dark implication kerneled within all art, and may, as is frequently so among artists, be without conscious knowledge. But I have noticed that when she performs this pantomime for our parents, the flight is confined to the middle of the room, is circular and lyrical and nowhere approaches a web. I believe, therefore, that the other version has contained all along a message, a plea, if you will, for me. But this belief began with my dreams and is retroactive. Our mother says that this act, performed without hurry and embellished each time with subtle and new inspiration, is as constantly surprising as a sunrise. Our father beams and tugs at his whiskers, saying, "Well, well!"

On evenings of the butterfly we part thoughtfully with whispered "good nights." But other evenings, when she has outraged, or so they pretend, the sensibilities of our parents with something ultramodern—even at times scatological—the partings are raucous and the twins have to be looked in on time and again and warned to be quiet. If it is a silent night of no wind and a cold moon, our mother says that our high spirits can be heard by the neighbors. Watching my sister's face, I see that "the neighbors" is a euphemism for the owl.

Anyone but my sister would find it strange that it is those evenings of high times that I have come to dread, when she, having been reckless in her invention, is dangerously wound up. Alone with her in her room when the others have finally gone to sleep, I am sole witness to where recklessness could lead her, for she does not act for my benefit. It is as though her sense of achievement wants not to be contained, wants to be carried afield. I have seen her—not oblivious to me, but trusting, which is a kind of oblivion—rake her nails against her low ceiling, at times savagely, as though to claw through to the world, but at other times with a rhythmic and terrible softness as though she were sending messages in code to a listener above, a lover with his breast and ear laid to her roof.

Scrabble scrabble—pause—scrabble scrabble scrabble. It is almost literally unnerving, for I can feel mine jumping along their length as though to tear through my skin, my nerves' roof. But I am no longer young enough to plead, to cry her name, squeaking like a baby. And what would I say? "Don't leave me, my dearest sister?" It would be a violation of our basic and necessary fatalism, and I can imagine a scornful reply or sore disillusionment, which would be worse.

She trusts me as an equal and this, I believe, led to my dreams and fostered my revelation. Does this make them artificial, the products of a deep wish to accommodate myself to her needs, her superior philosophy? My rejection of this may be less conviction than wish, again; I am a fledgling in the shadowy field of dreams and hunt there half blinded like the owl by daylight.

The last time my sister performed the butterfly, when the frost crackled about us and the earth creaked in the silences of her artistry, when she emerged from the chrysalis, unaware of her beauty, wondering at the sights and sounds of the world, it happened that the owl cried and it was as though he sat upon us, separated from us by no more than a membrane. For the first time in a dance my sister spoke. "How innocent you are! Look at you, how innocent!" My parents took this as improvisation, as a cry addressed to herself, the butterfly. But I saw that she spoke to change her face with words, to erase the expression that had lived there as though indelibly etched with acid. To hide herself from us, from me, she violated her art.

What I had seen on her face when the owl cried, in the moment before she became a talking butterfly, was passion. It was profane. I had finally isolated and defined the "something" that our mother and I regretted and that I feared immeasurably, having seen it. Did mother see, too? I could not ask.

That was the night I dreamed my sister, dreamed the owl, saw my sister drawn irrevocably to the door, saw the door open, the moon beyond. I woke with a shout, an outcry to frighten all but the owl. When the others had gone back to bed, our father grumbling to reassure us, I re-saw the dream while it was fresh and horrid, wiped out all extraneous detail and concentrated upon the look on my sister's face. Yes, it was profane, it was carnal, it was sexual. But at the door it changed. Standing under the open door with the hunter's moon, the moon-hunter, behind her, she turned as though to say good-by and the look said, clearer than words, "Be glad for me!" It said, "I know what I am, now."

To speak of revelations is difficult and dangerous, for there are would-be disciples waiting to misinterpret and misuse the dreams of others. Therefore I will be as plain as I can be and interpret my own dreams. Within the dream I was informed of this: dreams are given to us as projections of light from the parts of our brain to which no passage exists in the daytime, the corridors swollen with everyday thoughts and frets and wishes. In sleep these corridors contract, and philosophy and art emerge as themselves, for they would not be recognizable to the everyday brain of an average creature. Thus: in dreams we are all philosophers and artists. In sleep, I saw what my sister, the artist, sees in her waking hours, and I understood.

I did not wish to, do not wish to, and I do not accept it yet but I have seen within the radiance.

I ask myself: do I understand to the extent of not stopping her when the time comes that she is drawn to the door and upward, and I—we all are—wide awake and able to coax, to divert, if necessary, to restrain? My instincts are of no use. Our mother would not even understand the question, I feel. My father? Again, I do not know.

My conclusion: it would be best if it happened when we are all late at our hunting and my sister, who is forbidden to hunt at night in winter, is alone. I pray that it happens that way. We could not forget her, but if she were gone when we returned we would not *know*, and thus could keep her memory alive, however somberly, through speculation. We could avoid somberness by inventing travels for her, and successes in the wide world; we could tell each other that any day now, any night, she might reappear with gifts for the twins and tales to keep us up until all hours, and new pantomimes! Our mother could weave for us the colors and textures of the costume my sister would be wearing, and the jewels in her ears. I pray that she may, like another of us, simply not be there when we return.

And my dreams tell me further: there is something maiming about bearing witness to another's epiphany. Assuredly there is an owl in every life, but the terror, my dreams inform me, is that it will prove in most lives to be just that: an owl. I was advised that of all the humours, yellow bile, or envy, is the most destructive. This is the one dream that I cannot fathom at all.

In my latest dream my sister turns at the door, the moon behind her, and I see them as one. Then the owl is silhouetted against the moon, my sister, and they are a trinity. In any combination of pairs the sum is the third. It is like a Fibonacci sequence. This, I think, is a wishful dream, for if she were the owl I would not miss her, could bear to look at a future without her, would kill her if I could . . . Perhaps in an effort to join her, inseparably, I tell myself that the last clause above makes me, too, the owl.

In the meantime we are a happy family. I say it determinedly. Our home is snug. The remains of a nearby harvest are still plentiful. We do not have to go very far to gather grain and can best the low-flying owl by twilight, teasing his dazzled sight and ducking into our doorway and laughing; at least the twins laugh, for until the ground is hard frozen and the moon sits implacably pointing at our entranceway frost-buckled above ground, foraging and life itself are games to them.

The dreamers among us are learning to keep our dreams to ourselves. Lately my sister has sat with us in the evenings and when the owl gives its shivery cry she does not tremble but seems to grow drowsy with indifference. Our mother smiles and nods, her eyes confiding in me her relief. I nod back, and smile. Our father cracks corn for all of us, masticating it for the twins, for winter is upon us, moon and owl, and the corn is half frozen.

FOUR AUSTRALIAN POETS

LES A. MURRAY · GRACE PERRY ·
WILLIAM FLEMING · BRUCE DAWE

A selection edited by Noel Stock

EDITOR'S NOTE: *The change that has come over Australian poetry during the past fifteen years, whatever its immediate origins, owes a great deal to the liberating power of the so-called "modern movement" in English and American verse. Australian poets of an earlier generation, such as Robert Fitzgerald, Judith Wright, Kenneth Slessor, Gwen Harwood, and David Campbell, made their peace with the twentieth century, certainly; but they were not really within the "modern movement," whatever part that movement may have played in their work. Two of the most civilized Australian poets since the Second World War, James McAuley and A. D. Hope, knowing what they were doing, consciously planted their roots in the English poetry of the seventeenth and eighteenth centuries.*

But the poets of the past decade, on the other hand, including the four represented below, have been able to take the "modern movement" for granted. The two main streams which created the literary world in which they write (I do not speak here of direct influences) were: 1) the hallucinatory aspect of Symbolism, as represented by, say, Rimbaud and St.-John Perse; and 2) the American concern with native language and native places, as it may be found in a line running from Whitman through Pound and Wil-

liams to Charles Olson and Ginsberg. Contemporary Australian poets, taking these things for granted, seek to give voice, as unself-consciously as possible, to the things that interest them; they seek to write from where they are: to know the history of the place, or to catch the scene passing through the time and place in which they find themselves.—N. S.

LES A. MURRAY: FIVE POEMS

PENTECOSTAL

Coming away from a modern occasion, a man said:

In upper rooms, in brick-and-iron churches
other uprooted ones are also speaking
in languages that rip the shirt of nexus.

They're an utter offence to the unmerciful quotient
and they're not even a side. They surround the arena,
praising, with careful decorum. Not seeking known gains.

I was ground all my life between the levels of language,
by liberal English, our Worldspeak, that horrible binary
code of left/not-left, stylish/unstylish,

by managing jargons that set a heavy asphalt
on the grid of your life, with a bubbling of stale jokes,
by the speech of the shrewd, who starve in perfect cover . . .

I fled these so far I had to see through mushrooms:
you machinegun the family and take your Christmas presents.
The verbiage I smoked there was sharp stuff, half green.

At this level of reeling, I struck a door that answered.
It's hard to tell you amongst whom, in a language
that harbours the word "proletariat." Among very brave askers.

War or passion would never demand sharper
exposure than this, to abandon hard-kept dignity
the little he hath, under lights, in front of people

to abandon dear sense, like Byrd in the Antarctic
extinguishing that stove that warmed and poisoned him
to fall on the wholly unknown, the breadth of heaven.

And they are angels, of human-instinctive feather,
        these unassuming
verberations. Times lost and coming are in them.
I say human *angels*. Saints would be dressed in known words.

And socialism is merely a duty, like justice—
establish these before they bore us, he cried.
These tongues are a dawning Finnish in our jargons

they are Eloi and Ephpheta, the dark towers crumbling,
they are saying the name of Christ in glittering circles,
they are outermost rims of that Name, like flowering trees.

He walked, smiling shyly, like one holding in his music.

from SIDERE MENS EADEM MUTATO

It is some while since we roomed at Bondi Beach
and heard the beltmen crying each to each.
Good friends we made while snatching culture between
the cogs of the System (they turned slower then)
reemerge, and improve as their outlines grow more clear
(but where's Lesley now? and Jacqueline, what of her?)
Academe has grown edgier. Many still drowse in the sun
but intellect sounds like the cocking of a Sten gun.
Remember urbanity, by which our time meant
allusions to little-known Names in a special accent?
It persists—but war's grown; war, snarling out of that trip
in which Freud and Marx are left and right thongs in a goosestep.
Mind you, Jane Fonda plays in it too. It's fairly thin war.
The tiger is real, and in pain. He is fed on paper.

THE VERNACULAR REPUBLIC

I am seeing this: two men are sitting on a pole
they have dug a hole for and will, after dinner, raise
I think for wires. Water boils in a prune tin.
Bees hum their shift in unthinning mists of white

bursaria blossom, under the noon of wattles.
The men eat big meat sandwiches out of a styrofoam
box with a handle. One is overheard saying:
drought that year. Yes. Like trying to farm the road.

The first man, if asked, would say *I'm one of the Mitchells.*
The other would gaze for a while, dried leaves in his palm,
and looking up, with pain and subtle amusement,

say *I'm one of the Mitchells.* Of the pair, one has been rich
but never stopped wearing his oil-stained felt hat.
      Nearly everything
they say is ritual. Sometimes the scene is an avenue.

THE EUCHRE GAME

So drunk he kept it at tens—and the bloody thing lost!
he bought a farm out of it. Round the battered formica
table the talk is luck more than justice, justice
being the politics of a small child's outcry.

The subtlest eyes in the Southern Hemisphere look at
the cards in front of them. *Well I'll go alone.*
Outside the window, passionfruit flowers are blooming
singly together. Many are not in the sun.

Men lose a trick, deal a fresh hand. Intelligence here
is interest and the refusal of relegation;
those who conceive it chance-fixed to their benefit also
believe in justice. Some of them are what remains of

the Revolution. *Hey, was that for us?* Footsteps
recede down the hall. One looks at the window, three smile:
Europeans! you're all suffering-snobs. Who's away?
The game's loosely sacred: luck is being worked at.

LACHLAN MACQUARIE'S FIRST LANGUAGE

The Governor and the seer are talking at night in a room
beyond formality. They are not speaking English.
What like were Australians, then, in the time to come?
They had lost the Gaelic in them. It had become
like a tendon a man has no knowledge of in his body
but which puzzles his bending, at whiles, with a flexing impulse.
They'd wide cities, dram-shops, carriages with wings—
all the visions of Dun Kenneth. The singing at a ceilidh

lacked unison, though: each man there bellowing out of him
and his eyes undirected. *Had they become a nation?*
They had, and a people. A verandah was their capitol
though they spoke of a town where they kept the English seasons.

I saw different things: a farmer was telling his son
trap rabbits and sell the skins, *then* you can buy your
Bugs Bunny comics!—I didn't understand this. All folk there,
except the child-hating ones, were ladies and gentlemen.

GRACE PERRY: FIVE POEMS

ALCHEMIST

We have all suffered
hermetic transmutations
sin   ablution   passion

the final triumph is no ordinary gold
rather a hardening
the soft made solid
absolved from need   emotion   reaction
the son of Zeus deceived us
beyond our interpretation of salvation
into a suspended inhumanity
redundant sciences
undergo automatic involution
life under pressure dries out
only the gene endures
the microcosm takes over
order is reversed
lenses probe eyes
for the infinite image   the self inverted
organisms in suspension on glass slides
gaze up microscopes
condensing mirrored light
on man caught bending

MARTIN PLACE, SYDNEY

Regime on trial
and all my bright soldiers
melted in shell fire
even the pigeons have deserted
their customary coronets
the crusted shawls
in the sunless plaza
terror cut out the tongues of newsboys
confetti flower stalls
spill posies choked purple
no one is buried in the monument
the guardians sleepily
gaze at the steps
            grey columns
the white flakes
dropping through smooth brass mouths

SONG OF THE BIRDS

(Pablo Casals 24/10/73)

Pablo is dead
          as those birds
                    are dead
that sing to us
          now
             in this room
             of leaffall in spring
                evenings in Catalan
winterwhite sound
            trembling
                 olive trees
at the edges of oceans
            gathering
                birds
in a wide blue apron
            wet with tears
his hands
       his invisible wings
              restore them
      gentled and transformed
those blind birds
         remote beyond words
lamenting
      all deserted cities
           undefended
              open to death

CATCH THE GREASY PIG

Midsummer hands apply the oil
many have died for less
the crowd breathes in
white mouth bites green
I stand full circle of my universe

all my myths born in me
dreams of islands swing northern lights
through screams of oceans men foam forward
they do not know
                        the holy one
                        unclean   untouchable
spray bright bodies wilder than nine dancing women
moonfaces whirling widdershins
change   age   girl to crone
devouring the black brother
up skirt tunnels dark at noon
midwinter solstice
I shall not
grow the newmoon tusks of my father's father
I shall not
feed on flesh nor corpse meat
I am not
the child they seek
yet am I torn
and seared by succulent desiring
o golden she who weeps
o Ishtar   save me   let me die

MYTH

Zeus grown old
and unconcerned with victory
rides jetpropelled
towards the new Olympus
lulled by libations of ambrosia
and inflight movies
he does not see
the man erect
            arms outstretched
momentary measure of the world
another and another
                        sucked under

the blue eternal crawl of time
metropolis rampant
the hybrid monster
neck stretched horizon to horizon
the hundred serpent heads
warring with the stars
the many voices
human   animal   musak gone mad
talking in tongues
the bull   the lion   and the snake
out of the east
the flaming thunderbolt stops here
this time Typhon shall not be destroyed

WILLIAM FLEMING: A POEM

NED KELLY

Come all ye top dogs, fat cats, and other
sundry adherents of the cult of We Know Best:
hear the tale of one man who
wasn't impressed.

He came from a clan whose official attainments would
be better left unsaid;
his name—Edward Fitznolan Kelly,
better known as Ned.

The landscape he inhabited was hard—
barren, dry, and brown:
the kind that consistently and with complete predictability
turns you down;

not the place, indubitably,
for urbanised dittos:
a background, in short, that
was absolutely shithouse.

Whenever a safe was blown, a bank
hit, and particularly when
a patrol failed to report—you could count
on it: Kelly had struck again.

The fuzz were in despair, as were the upper
administrative echelons of every rank—
not to mention Cabinet, the P.M., and the Governor
of the Reserve Bank.

Even the President of the A.C.T.U.
was shit-scared:
no-one knew on whom would descend
his *blitz-krieg*.

Their problem: while most folk just
whine or shrug their shoulders,
Kelly instead to direct
action was emboldened.

He hadn't been ever "bad"; once
one of the listeners
he'd sat content like the rest of us just
minding his own business,

till one day when he struck in
person a power-addict
(I'm bigger than you are, so shut your face!),
to which he replied, Get nicked!

He couldn't help it; on the day when
he heard, Look, chum,
what I say goes 'cos I'm the boss,
straight he returned, Pig's bum!

What next was to do was plain: he
hammered an armour the same day;
could there thenceforth 'twixt him and them be
any *détente*? No way.

An inspiration he was to ordinary folk:
no wonder the big wigs set in
motion the State's machinery in their
efforts to get him.

But when the bulls came after him
with drawn guns and truncheons,
he shot them dead with-
out compunction . . .

Anyhow, one day he assembled his gang
so's to get them set
for a spectacular stroke the authorities 'd
never forget.

Me plan, he said, 's
t' take over Glenrowan—
the hall, stores, streets—in short,
bloody-everything goin'.

Youse two'll cut the railway while
quietly me an' Joe
'll sneak in the jailhouse—then
LET GO!

. . . And so they went. Kelly, buckling his
armour, spurred on his horse—Git up!
A blow at their infrastructure—this'll
make 'em sit up!

The surprise was total—as was
due such daring—
and before you could say Jack
Robinson they were Power-Sharing.

They set up headquarters in the local
pub. No-one came or went
or did anything without their permission—a
rival government!

In their euphoria, however, the possibility
of betrayal was forgotten:
big men do tend to forget
that people are rotten.

The question of internal security was
therefore not tackled:
the eternal betrayer was there: observed:
the telegraph crackled.

Thus word to the seat of power was
got through by the dobber;
the pigs went mad; you could almost
hear them slobber.

They descend in droves on Glenrowan,
and then (but not until
all escape-routes were sealed off) they
moved in for the kill.

Their plan? to set fire to the pub
—some stroke of brilliance!
(To stifle opposition,
they'll spend millions!)

This was the show-down, Kelly
knew. Surrender? —It didn't dawn.
With guns blazing he crashed
out—it was on!

At once in the greeting fusillade he
fell, his leg shattered.
Finished? —No! He got up and came
at them again. The johns scattered . . .

Bullets pinged from his armour . . .
Dozens of shots wasted . . .
But it couldn't go on; it just had to
happen . . . What a bastard!

Bleeding he lies, yet still they lack
the guts to grab him;
finally a platoon at gunpoint was
sent to nab him.

When they bore him to Melbourne with
clothes still soaking,
did the mob come rushing to save him? —You'd
have to be joking!

The turn-coat crowd in its affections
constantly zig-zags.
That's people for you—all
dags! *dags!* DAGS!

Flocked to his trial academics and commentators all
most cultured,
smothering the truth, as normal, in
self-gratifying bullshit.

Did it worry him?—No.
Let them, he thought, bask
in his glow if it helps them—no
skin off his arse! . . .

So they found him guilty, condemned
him to take the long trek;
then on the appointed day they
stretched his neck.

But Kelly, illusionless, had never been
one to gripe:
it's what he'd always expected: his
last words—Such is Life!

For that's how it is when you're
authentic, when you're ready to give
rather than keep: the mean-
minded won't let you live.

But remember this, pigs, from Moscow
to Westminster, from Capetown to New Delhi:
however obscene your precautions, always
there'll be a Kelly.

BRUCE DAWE: FOUR POEMS

ELEGY FOR DROWNED CHILDREN

What does he do with them all, the old king:
Having such a shining haul of boys in his sure net,
How does he keep them happy, lead them to forget
The world above, the aching air, birds, spring?

Tender and solicitous must be his care
For these whom he takes down into his kingdom one by one
—Why else would they be taken out of the sweet sun,
Drowning towards him, water plaiting their hair?

Unless he loved them deeply how could he withstand
The voices of parents calling, calling like birds by the
        water's edge,
By swimming pool, sand bar, river bank, rocky ledge,
The little heaps of clothes, the futures carefully planned?

Yet even an old acquisitive king must feel
Remorse poisoning his joy, since he allows
Particular boys each evening to arouse
From leaden-lidded sleep, softly to steal

Away to the whispered shore, there to plunge in,
and fluid as porpoises swim upward, upward through the dividing
Waters until, soon, each back home is striding
Over thresholds of welcome dream with wet and moonlit skin.

BEATITUDES

Blessed are the files marked ACTION in the INWARD tray,
    for they shall be actioned;
Blessed are the memos from above stamped forthrightly
    in magenta FOR IMMEDIATE ATTENTION,
        for they shall receive it;
Blessed are the telephones that chirrup and the marvellous
    conundrums conveyed thereby;
Blessed also the intercom calling this one or that from
    his labours that he may enter into the Presence;
Blessed the air-conditioning system bringing a single guaranteed
    hygienic weather within these walls;
Blessed the discrete articulation of management
    by whose leave the heart beats;
Blessed the barbiturate of years, the desk-calendar's inexorable
    snow, the farewells rippling the typing-pool's
        serenity, the Christmas Eve parties where men choke quietly

                                            over

        the unaccustomed cigar and the elderly file-clerks
          squeal at the shy randyness of their seniors;
Blessed the punch-card fantasies of the neat young men
    whom only the blotter's doodling betrays;
Blessed the complete liturgy of longing, the stubbed grief,
    the gulped joy, the straightened seams, the Glo-weave yes,
      the rubberized love, the shined air, the insensible clouds,
        the dream rain and see there over and above
          the rainbow's wrecked girders
            the pterodactyl smile . . .

THE DAY THAT THEY SHOT SANTA CLAUS

The day that they shot Santa Claus
money fluttered sadly from the trees,
cash-registers played Verdi's *Requiem*
and a diminutive orphan breeze

rose up from the credit columns of ledgers
and tinkled dolefully at each shop door
while the city's father-figure lay in mourning
in the bargain basement of a Bourke Street store.

The news spread like a darkness; in the bosoms
of sales-girls the little lights winked out,
chewing gum lost its flavour on the instant,
copy-writers felt the dramp of doubt.

Everywhere were testimonies to the violence
the natural order suffered; shepherds glowed
with more than ever their customary festive spirit,
reindeer ran amok in Sydney Road,

and from the sky—as from the vaster heavens
of Coles and Woollies, not to mention Myers
—a bio-degradable snow came drifting earthwards,
Yarra Bank angels shuffled into choirs,

and there, at 45 r.p.m., they sang a heart-felt
miserere to the suspiciously blurred stars,
tore up their song-books, snuffed their wind-proof tapers,
and trudged down-town to drown their grief in bars.

MORNING BECOMES ELECTRIC

Another day
roars up at you out of the east
in an expressway of birds gargling their first
antiseptic song, where clouds are
bumper-to-bumper all the way back to the horizon.

Once seen, you know
something formidable, news-worthy,
is about to happen, a gull hovers
like a traffic-report helicopter over the bank-up,

one-armed strangers wave cigarette hellos from their cars,
an anxious sedan's bellow floats above the herd
—the odour of stalled vehicles
wickedly pleasant like an old burned friend,
still whispering to you from the incinerator.

Broad day is again
over you with its hooves and re-treads,
its armies, its smoke, its door-to-door salesmen,
irrational, obsessed, opening sample-cases in the kitchen,
giving you an argument of sorts
before you have even assembled your priorities,
properly unrolled your magic toast
or stepped into the wide eyes of your egg.

BIOGRAPHICAL NOTES

BRUCE DAWE, born in Geelong, Victoria, in 1930, was educated at the
University of Queensland and University of New England (Armidale).
After working as a farmhand, millhand, gardener, etc., he spent nine
years with the Royal Australian Air Force, and is at present lecturer in
literature at the Darling Downs Institute of Advanced Education, Too-
woomba, Queensland. His books include *A Need of Similar Name*
(Cheshire, Melbourne, 1965; awarded Myer Poetry Prize, 1966), *An
Eye for a Tooth* (Cheshire, Melbourne, 1968; awarded Myer Poetry
Prize, 1969), and *Condolences of the Season* (Cheshire, Melbourne,
1971; winner, Dame Mary Gilmore Award, 1973).

WILLIAM FLEMING, born in 1928 in Melbourne, Victoria, is an admin-
istrator in the Australian Bureau of Statistics. He publishes intermittently
in "little magazines" in Australia and abroad.

LES A MURRAY was born in 1938 and grew up in the farming and
forest country of the New South Wales north coast. Educated at Sydney
University, he has been a translator of Western European languages at
the Australian National University and an officer in the Prime Minister's
Department. His books include *The Weatherboard Cathedral* (Angus &
Robertson, Sydney, 1969), *Poems against Economics* (Angus & Robertson,
Sydney, 1972), and *Lunch & Counter Lunch* (Angus and Robertson,
Sydney, 1974).

GRACE PERRY, born in Melbourne, educated at Sydney University, is a physician who has held several pediatric appointments. She is currently in general practice. Editor of the magazine *Poetry Australia* (Sydney), her books include *Frozen Section* (South Head Press, Sydney, 1967), *Two Houses* (South Head Press, Sydney, 1969), *Berrima Winter* (South Head Press, 1974), and *Journal of a Surgeon's Wife* (South Head Press, Sydney, 1975).

THE SYNDROME OF GILLES DE LA TOURETTE

An excerpt from the novel The Trials of Sir Maximov Flint

MARTIN BAX

"Fuck him," Sir Maximov muttered as he snatched the wodge of packets restlessly from where it had fallen to the ground. He should, he supposed, be grateful that in this bemusing country called America (United States of), somebody should do something as logical as deliver his mail to him when mostly one had to wrestle with those wretched mailboxes. But here in this grand block there was a janitor given the job of postman and round he came with the letters; only he wouldn't (typical American) bother to knock, he pulled the door open and with some cry like "Ugh" the letters ejaculated into the room. At least, thought Maximov, there might at last be a letter from St. Paul about that boy John Doe.

Here he was with most of his sabbatical leave gone and no further with his massive and terminal text *Law and Peace*. Electing criminology as his starting point—because of its relationship to his own training—here he was still labouring away on rape and now, turning back to the thick volumes before him, seduced away from that to the Syndrome of Gilles de la Tourette. It had occurred to Sir Maximov that rape, at least in a young adult, might be a special example of Gilles de la Tourette's and if that was the case rape should never be subject to the law at all.

Sir Maximov paused to consider his own last remark. "Fuck him"

—was that too an example of this particular type of syndrome? Making a note to question Corbett about swearing, he pushed aside the three heavy volumes of Tourette's *Traité clinique et therapeutie de l'hystère* (Paris, 1891 and 1895) and started sorting through his post, discarding the advertisements for psychosurgery, for the obese people's suicide club, for recipes for aphrodisiacs (homosexuals only), for beverages distilled from menstrual blood of Serbo-Croatian nuns, and for cars designed by a British science fiction writer which had a built-in computer psychiatrist, until finally he came to the letter from Damascus, the communication from St. Paul. He tore it open—ah, at last, some details on John Doe, the Kalamazoo rapist:—

I spent the first half of my life getting all messed up inside—turning into what we on the ward called a "cat-rat-dog."

The other half of my life was spent trying to straighten out, and a state hospital (Ionia) made that pretty hard to do.

I grew up going from one boarding home to another, becoming extremely hostile because, as far as I was concerned, my mother had forsaken me.

My father was never around, and yet I was always wanting him. My brother was older. He didn't seem like my brother. He seemed like just another person.

I don't remember it, but my doctors told me that the lady in the first boarding home where I was placed would lock me in a dark closet whenever I got lonely for my mother and acted up.

I was then about three years old. I was soon moved to another boarding home. I remember this one well. I loved the people who ran it. I guess I thought for a while that they were my real mother and father and I didn't want to leave when my parents finally came.

It wasn't until much, much later that I matured enough to realize that my mother hadn't rejected me. She had had tuberculosis and had been sent to a hospital for two years. Two years! It doesn't seem long does it?

By the time I was four or five years old, I had already closed out my mother from my emotional life. Then I shut out my whole family and eventually the whole world.

My feelings of rejection caused me to turn inside of myself. I gradually was filled with hate.

Every female was my mother. Everything that went wrong was a female's fault.

I got caught window-peeking, but they threw the case out of court.

Everything seemed like a nightmare . . . . trying to have relations with a woman and not succeeding, then trying to be a little boy and be cared for.

There was always the search to find someone to love me. There was always the wall or defense against being rejected. I never found anyone to love me.

When I was in my early teens, I broke into a place and hit a young girl on the head with a weapon.

They sent me to the University of Michigan's Neuropsychiatric Institute in Ann Arbor.

It was a big playground.

I was sixteen and already thought I was the butt end of everything in life. I was in a hospital to be cured, but my doctor, a neuropsychiatrist, made me feel worse. So many doctors, therapists, and social workers make their young patients feel inadequate.

I was released a couple of months later.

Back home, I got caught window-peeking and masturbating.

They sent me to another state hospital (at Kalamazoo). The pressures built until I exploded.

The patient who will be freed was identified in court only as John Doe. The patient was committed to Ionia State Hospital after raping and killing a student nurse eighteen years ago.

Eighteen years ago Sir Maximov had himself been called as a witness in his first "rape" case. And how many years before that had the unfortunate Valentine Baker, the hussar colonel, assaulted the righteous maiden in the railway carriage? Maximov's efforts to understand what the girl had said and done in that case had been hampered by the Colonel's upright behavior: Sergeant Ballantine had to fight a case against insurmountable odds because the Colonel, from a rare sense of chivalry, had absolutely refused to allow him to cross-examine Miss Dickenson. "I was debarred, by his express instructions, from putting a single question."

And here, curse him, Sir Maximov had another case where the rapist could tell him nothing about the behaviour of the raped female. "I don't remember much about what happened . . . . I broke down on the stand and was sent back to Ionia as a sexual psychopath." Wearily Maximov filed John Doe into his folder and penned a brief note of thanks to St. Paul: "but I need the details, *the details* of his original crime, where are they?"

Then back to Tome Two of Gilles's great work on hysteria: "*seconde partie—Hysterie Paroxystique avec 63 figures dans le texte et un portrait à l'eau-forte du professeur Charcot.*" But still no sign of a portion of the text describing that syndrome Maximov was studying and which was adorned by Gilles de la Tourette's own name . . . .

Locking his door carefully after securing all his files, Sir Maximov began to plan the route that would take him out of this great Law Emporium. He often wondered about his papers—suppose the President should ask to see them—he knew he would be arraigned at once and indeed he intended to be well out of reach of any lawyer before they were published, but the problem of how they were to be secreted out of this building and how a printer could be found who would set them remained unsolved. As to his present predicament—how was he to reach his lodging without being called in for jury service? His date with Wendy was set for seven, it was now six-thirty and surely some of the judges would have decided to suspend sittings for the day. He decided to plan his exit via level seven to the halfway mark and then use the janitor's stairs to get down to level three and then hope to make it to the service elevators without becoming involved.

The courts of level seven were relatively safe as far as the stairway, as they tried minor motoring offenses—damage to property, pedestrians, and parking offenses—and they were handled without juries, but beyond that were the serious offenses—incidents involving damage to other motor vehicles—here juries were impounded, hence the need to escape to lower levels rather than pass level seven section B. If only no lawyers who knew him emerged from the courts as he passed. But of course they all knew him now —"our tame psychiatrist," "he says he's not sure if there is any basis for law at all," and then roaring with laughter. If they hadn't thought him comic—"good God," thought Sir Maximov, "where would I be now!" He shut his eyes, still standing by his office door, and waited till Wendy was able to suppress all the other confusing images which were occupying his mind. It was easy to be back in their first cocktail party: he had thought the girl would come. He had seen her at the formal function the night before and watched her loping into the end of a conference session to look for her father. Jeans with neatly embroidered flowers and worn so much, much better than anything those fearful female lawyers could manage. Then at the private party her father—but no girl. Depression but—easy—late of course, she would be, and arriving looking slightly alarmed just when Max had slipped away from a group and was standing alone. "Can I get you a drink?"

Dinner (God, would his European Sabbatical Grant last)—fifty dollars he'd paid for the two of them and they were not even alone. All those others—Peter whom he'd had to talk to as they were stuck at the end of the table—so she rattled away to that dreary sociologist. But afterwards, O.K. . . . O.K. . . . not in your bed the first night but I like you and tomorrow night is free. A girl from the beaches—bronzed—teaching or something—so not dim but mainly being aware of her body. Hating this campus but loving her father. Poor man befuddled by it all—Judge on the Offshore Islands! The girl loving mirrors, wanting always to make love where she could watch it/him in the mirror.

Then . . . . "Maxy, just a moment, won't take a moment . . ." "No! Not jury service, I want you just in court a moment . . . . professional witness . . . . just to say nothing psychiatric in this behaviour." "Nice little case, obscenities in the foyer of level one. How about it? Maxy . . . ." He couldn't say no, so "all right, all right . . . ." Down into the well of the court and looking over at the dock, looking at the prisoner . . . . Wendy. Her staring back at him. Knowing it was going to be really good deep loving . . . . except she was the prisoner. And turning to look at the judge and the prisoner Wendy turning too and kicking over her chair with a violent spasm shouting at the judge a forceful expletive "Cunt!" Of course, easy, easy, relaxed, "My lud, for once my lud I think we can say clear-cut psychiatric evidence, a cut-and-dried case, my lud. No doubt about it, my lud, as I'm sure you'll agree when I show you the texts. A case, I say, a case, we call it a syndrome my lud, The Syndrome of Gilles de la Tourette."

By this time he had reached the janitor's stairway safely but when he got to level three and peered cautiously through the glass circle in the door he had seen a stream of lawyers passing and had shot back round the bend halfway up the stairs to level four and was busy readjusting his shoelace. The court had required that he reattend in a week's time with documents to support his proposal that Wendy had an illness. He would like to have Tourette's own text but there was plenty of recent literature. Corbett had kindly sent him his file on tics, and, with Corbett's special interest in this syndrome exemplified in half a dozen reprints, Sir Max felt he could keep any judge at bay. He intended to start with a straightforward textbook account. "A ticlike syndrome of violent bodily spasm presenting usually around puberty and associated with coprolalia and less commonly coprophagia."

The lawyers would not know what either of those words meant and when questioned he ought to be able to load secondary texts on them and discuss the derivation of the words for some hours. "Coprolalia my lud? Well, loosely, my lud, obscene speech (coprophagia, of course, obscene action) but we must look beyond this simple definition my lud, we must look to a deeper meaning and here, my lud, I draw your lordship's attention to Corbett, Mathews, Connell, and Shapiro, my lud, 1969 *British Journal of Psychiatry* . . . ." That reference alone would keep them twitching and he was sure the case would be postponed for study by the time he'd given them another five references . . . . yes, he should be able to get the case put back indefinitely. And then, make sure the police were not holding her passport and ship her back to the offshore island. But what would happen to him then in this insane country?

The swing door crashed open below him and the janitor shot through with bucket and mop. It was the same janitor who delivered the post and he started up the stairs and was almost beside Max before he caught sight of him. A violent spasm shook the man's body and caused him to jerk the bucket so that water flooded over Maximov's feet completely filling his shoes. "Lawyers," he shouted, "fuck 'em!" This was an epidemic; for Maximov realized in a flash that the janitor thought that he was a lawyer. As with Wendy, the sight of a lawyer triggered the attack. Maximov suddenly realized that the sound the janitor made as he shot the postal package through the door was not a guttural greeting but an obscenity—true coprolalia; and that the spasms which caused the letters to career into the room in that wild fashion were not caused by a violent conscious movement, they were a forced unconscious convulsion—a true tic—another sign of The Syndrome of Gilles de la Tourette.

THE YELLOW ROBE

A Travel Diary

U WIN PE

Self did not make me, nor self nor any other. Yet the notion of Self or self or some other made me. And with a body and mind caused this body and mind which will cause another body and mind so long as there remains the notion.

> from the ambulatory I can see
> beyond the tops of mango
> doorian and mangosteen
> the shoulder of a hill
> in the morning it is dim with ground mist
> in the afternoon it is blurred with haze

> walking beside the jasmine bush
> the mynahs do not heed me
> they cluck and whistle and flutter and hop
> and one flying in low from somewhere
> alights with a whirr of wings

> tea-dust swirl in the cup
> dark brown specks in amber liquid
> slowly drop to the bottom
> there they stay

Travelling the round of births of *samsara*. Treading the Eight-fold Path. Winning the Stream. Metaphors of Wayfaring. Incessant movement, there is no standing still. For one is not doing nothing at any time, one is always doing. And to do is to impel. So one goes—going on or getting out.

          jasmine and gardenia drench the walk
            with their delicate flavours
          I take 31 steps up this way
            and 31 steps down that way
          and 31 steps this way again

          let the assembly, revered brothers, hear me
            to whatsoever venerable it seems good
              let him remain silent
            to whomsoever it does not seem good
                let him speak
              to the assembly it seems good
                silent it remains
                  take it so

                head shaven
          carrying only the eight requisites
            the heavy robe somehow seems light
              as I take the first steps slowly
                from the Ordination Hall
                  onto the path

          salted boiled peas and plain hot tea
            to help this body get out of
          the low round table seating five
            body, sensation, and so on
          a small cloud passes quickly across
            the sky in the refectory window

            a round face in an aged head
          a low voice beneath soft words
              standing beside the coconut palm
                talking of pain and the end of pain
                    wayfaring

The life lived without awareness is the tainted life: tainted with
wanting, tainted with not wanting, tainted with not knowing about
the notion of Self and self. Awareness should be of each doing
every moment. Mindfulness is the watching and warding of aware-
ness.

> 4 a.m. the stream of breath
> 216 cycles per minute
> in-breathing, out-breathing, in-breathing
> watching the touch
> aware of sensation as it is
> airflow at the nostril tip

> the morning is noisy with birdtalk
> koels, jays, mynahs, sparrows, bulbuls
> I follow each song and twitter
> not koel shout, jay song, sparrow twitter
> but each note as it falls upon my ear

> the wind rises in the afternoon
> it ruffles the topmost branches of
> the doorian
> then it shakes it thoroughly
> raises a flurry in the almond tree
> flutters the window curtain
> and comes to me

> 9 p.m. mindful of sensation
> when sensation is full with mind
> and mind is full with sensation
> the bright green world beneath the waves
> at Set-se beach
> the sea is permeated with the one taste

Colours seen with the eyes closed are brighter than colours seen
with open eyes. Brighter than these are the colours seen when
the mind is brought to a point. But colours, lights and images are
distractions.

mango tree, sky, monastery wall
sun brings out the green
the blue, the white
and sunlight all bright yellow
on monk's robe hanging out to dry

lights are a curtain hiding Light
lights are a turn-off to delight
lights are bright colours
not hot but cool
lights are a pleasant quiet pool
lights do not light the way to ardour
lights are a curtain hiding Light

The end of the world is not reached by travelling. Within this fathom-length body with its sense-impressions, thoughts and pains, is the world, the making of the world, the ceasing and the way to the ceasing.

inside this cell
sleeping, sitting, walking
reading, thinking, praying
meditating
better to look
inside this body

several fields west of the monastery wall
one under paddy, one under melon
one under peas
a speckled bull grazes there during the day
this body my grazing-ground

it goes from field to field
feeding indiscriminately
on straw, duckwort, poison weed
browsing here or lying there
chased by men with sticks in the field beside
the road
pelted by boys with stones in the water-meadow
rope it with in- and out-breathing
tie it to the hitch-post pain

No pain, no gain. This banal expression describes what is so but we would take it metaphorically. There is no path that has no pain. Pain is the stumbling-block or the stepping-stone.

      the aching inner muscle of the thigh is pain
    the thin thread of sharpness along the bone is pain
       the burning hands is pain
      pain is the general tone of discomfort
         only pain is
     or that which we have named pain

     it is not the hardness of floor plank
      which hurts
     it is the softness of my foot
      pain is not in the wind
     it is in the bones, the hands
      pain is in the mind

   discomfort from sitting too long on the floor
     the bother of setting out in the sun
       to retrieve the robe
     vexation from holding the book too long
   displeasure from thinking about the task
             to be done
     pain from meditation exercise
     unease is the common element

We err by naming that which is itself. We err by clothing the world in concepts. Knowing happens in time present and not by reaching before and after. Knowing happens in its own way.

     I say this robe this mat this razor
      this alms bowl
   this water-strainer this needle and thread
     this over-robe
     but pain is

    a jay sits daily on the almond tree
     it whistles several phrases
   whom is it telling all that to
   how to watch the pain in my ankle
     as it is without saying

in present pain is birdsong and jasmine
in present pain is the cup of hot tea
in present pain is the wind in the afternoon
in present pain is the shoulder of the hill
in present pain is the path through the orchard
in present pain the cup of tea is smashed

   drawing water
the well is wide and shallow
I draw a bucketful and put it in the tub
another bucketful and put it in the tub
   14 buckets and the tub is filled
getting to know is not filling a tub

Joy does not come through pleasure, joy comes through pain.
Agitation accompanies pleasure. The way to stillness accom-
panies pain. The end of pleasure is dissatisfaction. The end of pain
is joy. Then comes whatever has to come in its own way.

   a set of sharp knives
turning and turning in the ball
   of my ankle five days now
     suddenly
it went away this morning
     joy

   this flesh hung on these bones
   and knit with nerves
I have seen shredded
   and dropping
like great cliffs falling

   flesh is not solid
sunbursts burn at every pore
   no arms no thighs no legs
only the play of electricity
   vanishing in small flashes

the monk on my left
the coming does not make him glad
is the monk on my right
the going does not make him sad
gruel is food, boiled peas is food
hot tea is food.
pain comes and goes, joy comes and goes
sun in the morning, stars and moon at night
unattached

novices planting a jackfruit tree
9 years before the first fruit
they laugh and quarrel and banter
to them the world is trees and food and walking
the world is trees and food and walking

One sets out to arrive. One fares as one should. Arrival is in accordance with its own nature and in its own way. One sets out and goes on faring.

not a garden of roses and junipers
nor a valley of lilies
not a palace with cool drinks in the windows
nor a moon and a finger pointing
not the path through an orchard
to the shoulder of a hill
but a journey across hot sands
to a river

a small cloud moves in the southern sky
the morning breeze carries a wetness of river water
namo Buddhassa

TWO STORIES

WILLIAM S. WILSON

FATHERHOOD

I can't agree that the operation was as impossible as my colleagues now say. None of the objections is medical or biological, all are merely psychological, if not psychopathic. In no sense did the operation fail except that no donors were forthcoming.

The history of the operation is simple. Early work in the generation of one animal from the embryo of another by immersion in the morphogenetic field led to the possibility of regeneration of a human limb by creating a simulation of the morphogenetic field of the limb, a mesh of forces which would guide cellular development to construct an arm or a leg. If the first attempts were crude, later improvements in morphogenetic holography enabled doctors to regenerate arms or legs which were, through four-dimensional reversal, identical with the existing arm or leg which provided the template of the holographic field. The result was a greater bilateral symmetry than is possible in ordinary unsophisticated growth, and an unexpected dividend. The increased symmetry in children, subtle as it might seem, has resulted in different bodily experiences, and therefore in different feelings for symmetry in imaginative constructions. This so-called Dirac effect is yielding novel intuitions in particle physics and in zygotic algebra, for symmetrical scientists now define the evolution of the cosmos and the evolution of life both as a chain reaction of seriatim asymmetries. There is reason to hope that a mathematically gifted physicist, with regenerated and therefore symmetrical arms and legs, could achieve a unifield theory. Matter and energy may yet be understood as successive asymmetries of primal symmetrical space.

The benefits of the operation have appeared in topological mythography, where one of our own patients has recently demonstrated that as the myths of North America are to the myths of South America, and the myths of Europe are to Africa, so are the myths of North America to the myths of Africa, and the myths of South America to the myths of Europe. The beautiful result of these isomorphisms is that all of these myths and their interrelations can be mapped onto the Chino-Indian myth of Kuan Yin, a process which clarifies the shaping forces of our society. Advances almost as important have been made in psychology, where feelings, now defined as vectors, have yielded to description in a scalar-tensor notation. If the direction and force of feelings can be altered, perhaps I will have a donor yet.

My operation may have lacked something in original genius, but it had, and still has, some creative daring. The plain fact is that more boys are born without penises, or lose the penis as the result of a burn during circumcision, or as an accident of war, than is publicly admitted or popularly realized. The solutions are grotesque: to rear the infant boy as a girl, with virtuoso operations, injections of hormones, the danger of siloxanic poisoning, and rarely the possibility of orgasm or pregnancy. Such phantom women haunt the halls of medicine, and their existence may satisfy some doctors who, suffering vicarious death so often, might long for vicarious life. But the operations are a farce. The doctors who create such hybrids should take a good look at themselves and at their irrational fear of holographic regeneration.

The operation for the regeneration of a penis could not work with holographic reproduction of the morphogenetic field, for the organ was missing and could not provide the template. Yet the powers of regeneration have been discovered to be so strong, and the importance of the penis to manhood is so obvious, that an operation had to be invented.

The first solution, certainly not my suggestion, was to make the holographic field plates from the father. This was of course a narrow and reductivist conception of a biomorphic field and the first operations were butchery, with the child fitted to the templates of his father's field, and his hopes, if he were old enough to understand, raised only to be disappointed. The field of one individual cannot be grafted onto the field of another. The idea of a field transplant derives from a failure to comprehend field. Every problem of medicine is a problem of language, and this operation was a malapropism.

My solution was, and I still say is, classical and elegant. The simple operation entailed only the transplant of the organ of the father onto the son, after making holographic field templates of the father, and then regenerating a penis not on the child, who would then have his father's penis, but on the father-donor. All the father has to give his son is his penis and a few months of his time while he grows a new one. Such regeneration presents no difficulties, as we have shown with adult males such as soldiers who have providentially pre-filed the templates of their morphogenetic fields. The only failure occurs when there is some tampering with the field, as in the warpings of old templates. The plates for the father-son operation would be fresh, since they would be made immediately prior to the operation. The number of failures would be statistically insignificant.

I will not write defensively about this operation. My theory needs no defense, and my successful practice in generating arms and legs speaks for itself. The onus, if there is any, lies on those fathers who are asked to participate in an operation which has many beneficial side-effects for themselves. If anyone but the father could be the donor, medical authorities would be indifferent, but the chances for rejection of the transplanted organ are too great. The reasons for the refusals by the fathers I leave for them to state, hoping only that they will be honest and imaginative in examining their vectors. The complaint that the regenerated penis would not be circumcised is trivial and unworthy in discussion of an operation devised to relieve great suffering.

I do not think it too much to assume that, just as symmetrical mathematicians have different experiences of bodily geometry, and have mapped the bone-space of the body onto physical space with beautiful practical and theoretical results, so the son of a father who had donated his penis to him would have different bodily experiences, and a different genital space as a clue to the structure of existence, even as he would have living proof of his father's vectors. The perplexing implications are there, waiting for psychologists to unfold them. Think what might have been thought by the mind of Sigmund Freud who either had the transplanted penis of his father or who had made this gift to the manhood of his son. And think also of the pathos of the fact that we shall never know what could be felt by a son who had been made a gift of his father's penis, or for that matter, what could be gained by the father who made the gift and grown a new one.

MOTHERHOOD

As awkward as it is for me to write in defense of the operation that bears my name, I do so moved by the criticism that the operation is superficial because it is on the skin and for the sake of youthful beauty. I am aware that I was attracted to morphogenetic dermatology by the fact that few people died of skin disease. Perhaps that was cowardly of me, but suffering from pimples is as painful as any other suffering and I have found that cures for the skin are often cures for unhappiness. I wasn't merely doing cosmetic surgery on the vain or the rich. and any cowardliness in becoming a dermatologist is more than offset by the courage of my operation. The criterion of beauty in science should also support my work, not because the operation restores physical beauty, but because the operation is beautiful in its elegance and simplicity.

While I don't ask for or expect the approval of physical scientists, I do think that their own self-interest would require them to support my work. For the object of my operation is not merely the amelioration of suffering caused by the disfigurements of aging, it is a proof of field as the principle of biological development. Before morphogenetic regeneration, field was either a metaphor from magnetism with no satisfactory operational definition, illustrated by photographs of iron filings, or field was a concept used by mathematical physicists to get rid of infinities which they could not tolerate in their equations. Now field can be defined operationally and is a concept that a child could understand.

I have in other places acknowledged Dreisch as the father of morphogenetic regeneration. His early work retains the freshness of a great discovery, and it lives encapsulated in the contribution it makes to the assumptions and procedures of our more sophisticated work. When Dreisch showed that a single cell from the embryo of a sea urchin would grow into another embryo, he was dry and factual at first, but gradually he realized that a few facts about morphogenesis destroyed deterministic theories, which were based on the picture of the growth of crystals. Deterministic theories collapsed when it was shown that a cell could develop along any one of many paths. The morphogenetic field is the total of such paths. The landscape in which the cell grows determines the path that it takes, and this landscape can be simulated in modern holographic medicine. The cell lives in a field of criss-crossed opportunities, and its development is guided by the opportunities open to it. Anyone who has performed in a school laboratory the classical experiments on sea urchins and newts has seen the shaping power of the morphogenetic field.

Sea urchins and newts are less my problem than aging faces. I find no reason to think that aging is genetically determined. Genes do not provide information for the development of the individual beyond growth and the reproductive process in which the genes are transmitted to the next generation. Once past the reproductive stage, the individual has served the purposes of preservation of the species, and from then on he is on his own. The wrinkled human face is the victim of gravity and of cumulative errors in the reproduction of cells. Since aging is not programed, but is a badly improvised interference with youthful beauty, we have improvised an operation to counteract its effects. Aging is a form of misinformation. If we get the facts right, you will be able to read it in our faces.

I am not going to state for you the conclusions I have drawn about life while meditating on the faces I hold in my hand as I unwrap the bandages. I would rather describe the process of discovering the operation, which was almost accidental. I thought, while studying the faces of aging men and women, and while studying the science of morphogenetic development, that it might be possible to regenerate the human face. I was thinking of using templates made in youth to reorganize the cells of the sagging face into their earlier configurations. Toward this end, I was making templates of the morphogenetic fields of the faces of young women. We now know that such reversibility is impossible, and that the correct solution is, as it had to be, the simplest.

In thinking about the possible regeneration of faces, and in reasoning about embryology, I feared that I was dividing my attention, but then I could feel my separate interests converging toward a solution, as though guided by the undiscovered idea toward the idea itself. I knew I was near a solution without knowing what it was, and I had only to look into the eyes of a thirty-nine-year-old woman patient who chanced to be in my office—her ostensible problem a large naevus, but with two other problems —a wrinkled face and an unwanted pregnancy—and I saw the combination of my two interests and her two problems into a single solution: to use the cells from her embryo to regenerate her face.

When that moment returns to memory, I feel the idea hit me with the force of a physical object. The solution I had been looking for had found me. The operation had only to be seen there where it already existed as an objective possibility, although perhaps I had constructed my path toward the discovery by preparations which I had unwittingly made. My pleasure in the discovery is enhanced by the fact that I was not thinking about science or fame at that moment, I was simply feeling compassionate toward my patient.

I was not ready to operate on her. I diagnosed a shortage of zinc and referred her for collagen therapy. Then I took a leave of absence from the hospital and set up an abortion clinic on a Caribbean Island where the religion was opposed to abortion, the government indifferent, and the natives quite ready to supplement their magic with free health care. I had to learn, by trial and error, the appropriate moment in pregnancy to ablate the fetus, to shred it into a sterile nutritive medium in which the cells could grow, and then to transplant the growing cells into the face which had been prepared by removal of the epidermis and dermal fat. At the present stage in the successful development of our operation, the last difficulty is credibility—a forty-year-old woman returns from a Caribbean holiday with skin like that of a child.

In theory the use of the fetus should be possible for the father as well as the mother, but the theory hasn't worked out so well in practice. In the native population, where it was sometimes difficult to identify the biological father, the problem was to be expected, but the same difficulty has been encountered with white American fathers. There may be a hormonal problem in the father that does not arise in the mother because of changes owing to pregnancy. These are difficult problems, but I like to say that our problems are more valuable than most doctors' solutions.

The attempt to use the fetus on the face of someone in the family beside the mother has usually failed. The causes are not known. It is awkward to have an occasional inexplicable success, such as we have had with two grandmothers and three maternal aunts. In one of our most interesting cases, the fetus from a twin was used successfully on the patient and her twin sister, who looked even more alike after the operation.

There has been criticism that women have become pregnant in order to have the operation. The best answer to this charge is to admit it. Yes, they have. The practice is justified because of the need to schedule the operation so soon after conception. Certain knowledge of the time of conception is important. Mistakes were made until this point was understood, and anything that helps to establish the precise time is justified.

The charge that I have played a role in these conceptions I will not dignify with a reply. These charges are diversions by the entelechists who will say anything to discredit my work. At least they do not underestimate its importance as a refutation of teleology. My relation to my patients is professional, although paternal. A positive attitude in the patient toward herself is therapeutic, and a fatherly air of approval is good medicine.

The woman who undergoes this operation can sense the morphogenetic field at work in her face. She can feel the lines of force as they guide the embryonic cells into the patterns they must form. Why should a woman let her life be determined by tired collagens or by a shortage of zinc which weakens her electromagnetic field, the matrix of life. The goal of life is living. Life is a field of opportunity, guiding the individual forward along paths created by the meshed forces of objective possibilities as they interweave with a person's own potentialities. And this philosophy of life is now bodied forth in the faces of beautiful women.

A note on Lesbian women. The problem of women who want the benefits of the operation but not the experience of impregnation by a man has led to an improvement available to all women. One solution is artificial insemination, but the solution with scientific elegance is fetal transplant. We have a single continuous operation in which the patient is hypnotized into deep sleep, a fertilized ovum is transplanted into the ovary and allowed to develop, and then the embryo is ablated and shredded while the patient's face is prepared. The prolonged sleep shortens the period of convalescence. Time spent sleeping at the beginning of the operation is regained at the other end in rapid recuperation, so that any loss is made good with interest.

A FAIRY TALE OF
THE LAST OF THE BOARDGAMES

Or, The True Story of Pegasus

RÜDIGER KREMER

Translated from the German by Breon Mitchell

positions assumed
as usual
and the first ten moves asleep
: forays into no man's land
controlling space
for later manoeuvres

drawn in
striking from ambush
or unprotected
in advanced posts
waiting breathlessly
to be sacrificed for position
according to iron rules
and plans that no one understands
attacked or attacking
bound to fixed paths upon the field
in the same unchanging gait
: one forward one diagonal

battling
to be beaten
has long since become tiresome to him

in an unattended moment
he sneaks off
he deserts
he flees
the eight x eight = sixty-four squares
of boxwood and ebony
he dares
as if he had been bumped
to leap from the table
and falls upon the carpet

there he lies for a while as if dead
expecting
his absence to be noticed at any moment
to be located and picked up
placed once more in fortified positions
ready to carry out lofty plans

he pulls himself together
and hurries away
in broad leaps
hopping one forward one diagonal
across the black and red pattern of the carpet
to the door

through the hand's breadth opening
he springs out
and across the hall
tiled in yellow and brown
in accelerated gait to the stairs
he tumbles
pell-mell to the bottom
and finds himself
half stunned
upon the sidewalk

takes a deep breath
and straightens up
and snorts
and shakes his head
nothing appears to be broken
just a bit dizzy
he starts on his way
: grey on grey
the plastered sidewalk
but in squres all the same
: so he is able to get his bearings

hops upon the cobblestone street
close to the gutter
in order to be able to conceal himself
under leaves and paper
hidden
he waits breathlessly
for the strange noises to recede
by this means he advances
as twilight descends
to the edge of the city
and the broad blacktop highway
up into the mountains
: now it's all over
now there's no way to go on
now there are no more squares
no lines and no boundaries
everything is shapeless grey
now he can go no further in his peculiar gait
now there's no more one forward one diagonal
now the only way is straight ahead
so he springs straight ahead then
and again and again
can not understand
: it's so simple
to be something else

he must think this over
the rooks
the bishops
the pawns
: all of them could change completely
(for why should he alone be the exception to the supposed rule)
the queen in her terrible multiplicity
might all at once be completely helpless
at their mercy
the king in his lonely defense

the knight hopping in circles

: so the system is only an illusion
he must return
to tell the others
show them
how it is done
yet : no : how
does one hop in a circle on the square of squares
: one forward one diagonal

so he refutes himself
the dreamer
and no one will believe him
the liar
and no one will follow him
the rebel
out
onto the gridless surfaces
now he could talk and talk
for no one knows more
thoughts come tumbling forth
but words
are not found
to describe the reality
to express the truth
tentatively (to begin with)
just for himself
and all at once he feels lonely

and the pangs of hunger and thirst
and weariness
he would like to sleep now
and dream
of blossoming trees
and meadows just turning green
of a herd of black and white horses
in freedom
he dreams

: that refuge is no longer offered by
the may-green mixed forest
has long since been surrounded
by the king's troops
the pawns penetrating
arranged in open order
into the cracking underbrush
cover the deserter with leveled weapons
and bind him
to thwart any attempt at escape
the commander of the detachment announces
that they will fire immediately
without warning
the captured escapee is
turned over
directly to the authorities
until the trial
he is incarcerated
an inmate in solitary confinement
in the box
of polished ebony
he awaits the verdict and its enforcement
: death by firing squad

arrival of the detachment
advent of the prison transport
leading forth of the manacled deserter
binding of the condemned to the execution pole
positioning of the firing squad
deposition of the arms
distribution of live ammunition
final examination of the delinquent by the medical officer
injunction against photographs
check of the execution area
dismissal of nonparticipants
notification of readiness given to the king
reading of the order of execution
binding of the eyes of the condemned
final consolation from the military chaplain
king's order to carry out the sentence
execution
certification of death
(coup de grâce administered by the commander if necessary)
notification given to the king of sentence fulfilled
coffining of the corpse
order with respect to secrecy
departure of transport
assembly of detachment
clearing of the execution area
removal of all traces

he is awakened by the noisy birds
and shivers
in the falling dew
he grazes
in a clearing in the forest
the morning sun warms him
he throws his head back whinnying
and starts off
and makes his way
against the west wind

in the bright harsh midday light
a barricade blocks the highway
and opens the path
to inaccessible
fenceless meadows
soft green
fanned by sea wind
he rears up in revolt
and leaps at the barrier
(even if he breaks his neck trying)
now the base splinters
and the bonds break
and his legs are free
and his hooves strike sparks on the stone
he soars over

there
in the meadow by the sea
he meets a little fallow mare
still half a filly
rubs his cool nose
in the warm soft coat
feels her velvet lips
nuzzling caressing
his smooth ivory body
now a white coat grows upon him
and a magnificent tail
and a strong member
full of tender lust
he covers the mare
and conceives a son with her

he might live in the everglades
a quiet friend of the flamingos
the alligators
fear the blow of his hooves
and flee from the lagoon
into deeper waters
at night
he stands motionless
in the rustling reeds
a source of sustenance and consolation
for the mosquitos
he holds his tail in check

and farther away
across the sea
leaving the beacon lights behind
the foghorns buoys and signals
to the islands beneath the wind
or up to the klondike
(palms in the trade winds or gold beneath the snow)
he gallops
into the surf
his white mane floating like froth
and the waves breaking over him
now he sprouts wings

across the fine line of the horizon
into the cloudless
blue-black heavens
up to the stars
beyond the pleiades
then past aquarius and cassiopeia
he finds his place as
a fifteenrayed shining image
: pegasus

THE ENGLISH GARDEN

WALTER ABISH

One page in the coloring book I bought showed details of the new airport, the octagonal glass terminal building to the left, and a Lufthansa plane coming in for a landing in the background. It is a German coloring book and the faces accordingly are coloring book faces, jolly faces, smiling and happy faces. By no means are they characteristically German faces. Nothing is intrinsically German, I suppose, until it receives its color.

It could be said that the coloring book accurately depicts almost everything that could be said to exist in the mind of a child, and thousands of children each day gravely apply a color to each face, to each item, to everything that fills a space on the pages of the coloring book in much the same way that it occupies, visually at least, a space in real life.

When one is in Germany and one happens not to be German one is confronted with the problem of determining the relevancy and to a certain extent the lifelikeness of everything one encounters. The question one keeps asking oneself is: How German is it? And, is this the true color of Germany? Looking at the sky one is almost prepared to believe that this is the same sky that the Germans kept watching anxiously in 1923 and 1933 and 1943, that is when they were not distracted by the color of something else. Something more distracting, perhaps. Now the sky is blue. In German the word is *Blau*. But there are numerous gradations of blue . . . numerous choices for every child . . . The French say *bleu,* and we say *blue*.

The box of crayons I bought is also made in Germany. They resemble the crayons that are made in America, in France, and in Japan. The man waiting for me at the airport could easily have been any one of half a dozen happy-looking individuals on the second, third, and fourth pages of the coloring book. A trench coat slung over one arm. The shoes shined. He had spotted me at once. Speaking a halting but correct English he greeted me warmly. He smiled, hand extended. I touched a smooth dry palm.

The man who came to meet me doesn't drive the car. He sits at my side speaking about his recent trip to Belgrade . . . occasionally he interrupts himself to point to some distant object on the landscape. I obligingly turn my head to look in the direction he is pointing. He wears a well-cut brown pin-striped suit. A sedate businessman's suit. The chauffeur up front wears a uniform. It is a deep green. A forest green. The color of the Black Forest? The sky is overcast. The Mercedes is a dark brown. It is a German vehicle, superb, reliable and safe. That is not to say that there are no road accidents. Anything can happen on the road. A flat tire, a driver's miscalculation. But these occurrences are not kept hidden from the general public, on the contrary . . .

In the coloring book there are also illustrations of highways that resemble this one almost in every single detail. Nothing has been left out. There it is, the wide asphalt-covered highway that enables the automobiles and the trucks to cover a great distance at a fast clip. We are doing seventy. All around us other cars, Audis, BMWs, VWs and Mercedeses, are heading in the same direction, into the sun. Many of the cars contain families on their way home from a Sunday outing . . . faces colored various shades of satisfied red. Cheerful faces, massive faces, glum faces . . . It is late afternoon. They've had their walk. Their leisurely cup of coffee. They've taken a few breaths of the country air. *Fabelhaft. Hervorragend.* It was worth every minute of the drive. Definitely. It paid off. Definitely.

Everyone I speak to points out that living in Brumholdstein is so convenient. One is, in a manner of speaking, living in the country with all the conveniences that only a city can provide. And only twenty minutes away by car is the country. Only twenty minutes away and one can see cows and horses, brooks, farmhouses, barns, pastures, and people from another century. It'll take them, whoever they may be, at least another twenty years of building to wipe out the country . . .

The German signs on the grass, on the streets, on the highways, at rest stops are there to alert the traveler, just as in the coloring book the same signs are replicated to alert the child of the life that will soon engulf it. Yes, page after page of everything the child can ever hope to see. Tranquil domestic scenes, picturesque landscapes, Papa, Mama, and little Rudi hand in hand strolling in the woods, boarding a Lufthansa plane, visiting the zoo, rowing on a lake, serenity, ah, nature . . . eating at a restaurant, visiting a sausage factory, and joining the modern German army. How exciting, a landscape filled with quaint little stores, gasoline stations, hotels, bookstores, and railroad stations. Here and there a short stout man lifts a stein of beer. The country, according to the coloring book, is once again bursting with activity, a deep compressed energy that on every page displays a space for the color that will become its driving force.

It occurs to me that several pages of the coloring book could easily have been intended to depict parts of Brumholdstein where I am staying. With a few minor alterations it could quite easily become Brumholdstein. And why not. Perhaps the designers of the coloring book had Brumholdstein in mind when they designed the book. Brumholdstein named after the greatest living German philosopher, Brumhold. Somewhere in the coloring book his replica can be seen lecturing to a class. Written on the blackboard behind him are the words: What are we doing today? The philosophical implications of this sentence may be lost on the students, who are only eight or nine years old at the most. This in turn would make it unlikely that the elderly man behind the lectern is Brumhold. Nevertheless, by focusing on the professor and excluding the rest of the class, one can almost hear Brumhold speaking in his quiet controlled low voice, a voice that is also capable of expressing deeply felt emotion, for instance when Brumhold speaks of the many many Germans who, following the First World War, seem to have in the confusing process of what we call history lost their homeland, or at least a section or slice of it. A process, it might be added, that was repeated after the Second World War. The professor could be Brumhold, but he isn't. Brumhold retired years ago. By now he's an old man. He no longer lectures to young Germans. He spends his days thinking and writing . . . writing about why humans think, or fail to think, or try to think, or flee from thought, thereby inducing everyone who reads or tries to read his rather difficult books to think about whether or not they were really thinking or just pretending to think.

Brumhold is not the reason why I am in Germany, but his provocative questions may have been, without my being aware of it, an additional inducement to visit the country where Brumhold's metaphysical questions first saw the light of day. After all can one, to quote Brumhold, divorce the pleasure of being alive, of traveling in a foreign country, experiencing new sensations, from the very process of meditative thinking. Brumhold writes of the profound need and urge to *think*, and in a sense one must acknowledge that the Germans have always had a penchant for meditative thinking, a form of thinking that may sometime have verged on brooding. The language they speak has helped them immeasurably to shape their questions, and also enabled them to ask: What is this thinking all about? A question that did not hamper them from successfully building roads and new cities, cars and typewriters, both within the present boundaries of Germany as well as beyond those boundaries.

Still, metaphysics aside, Germans are a pleasure-loving people. They are the first to admit it. They have a word for pleasure, a word for bliss, a word for gratification, a word for rapture, and a word for ecstasy. They also, like the Americans, have a deep and abiding belief in perfection. The perfection of a well-built table, for instance, or a comfortable armchair, or a well-designed city, an attractive park with picnic tables and large shade trees, or a powerful motorcar engine, a formica-topped counter, or the white enamel coating of a pot.

One can see, from examining the people depicted in the coloring book, that all they need is a bit of color to come to life and embrace each other, and then in the best of humor, stroll over to a nearby café and have a *Bratwurst* or some other kind of *Wurst*, and then, to top it off, see a good film, a satisfying film shot in bright color, the bright color of Germany around them, the color that still remains to be added to these pages, the color that in the film isolates details, the details whose sum is perfection . . . a thought-provoking perfection . . .

Brumhold likes to draw a distinction between calculative and meditative thinking. Fortunately, as far as a child is concerned nothing that is depicted in the coloring book will force them to think in either one or the other manner. Whoever fills in the color can indulge in a little bit of both.

I love meditative thinkers, said Ingeborg Platt.

Naturally, insofar as any thinking is involved in a technological society, the preference by far is for calculative thinking. It determines the rate of growth in a city, the time it will take to install a pane of glass, break into a bank, paint a mural, compose a twelve-tone symphony, and ask oneself: Who is the stranger on the third floor?

I am the stranger.

What is he doing here?

At present he is contemplatively washing his hands. The soap is German. So are the gleaming faucet and the white basin. The white tiles on the floor and walls are also German, and so are the window frame and the glass and the shower and the bathtub and the view from the bathroom. In the coloring book, it must be pointed out, these details, these objects, these *things* are merely outlines. A child will see the outlines of the bathroom with eyes that can still accept the universality of all bathrooms.

In the coloring book, people, everyday sort of people, go about their everyday sort of life, absent-mindedly washing their hands, brushing their hair, eating their lunch, driving a car, trimming an occasional hedge, the coloring book functioning as an indicator and recorder of all things that are possible. But it is the possible that will never arouse anyone's disapproval. The coloring book simply activates the desire of most people to color something that is devoid of color. In this particular instant it is the normal every-day activity of people in the process of going about their tasks: feeding the dog, the baby, the husband, the tropical fish, them-selves, thereby acknowledging a need, not necessarily questioning the need, although they may ponder why . . . why must they feed the tropical fish and the baby and the husband. This in turn leads people to question other things. Why are the workmen at work on another library.

What is the man doing on the third floor?

He is making a local phone call. He is speaking to the Mayor of Brumholdstein. Naturally, the Mayor knows that I am here. He has been expecting my call. He knows where I am staying. He knows the house, the street, and other less pertinent details, for instance, he knows the dimension of the sewerage pipe, the width of the balcony, the number of stairs leading to the third floor where I am staying. He has a good head for details. He speaks an ex-cellent English. What's more, he enjoys speaking English. He enjoys saying: You must come over and have dinner with us to-morrow . . . and, I hope you like tropical fish . . . and, Do let me know if there's anything I can do to make you more comfort-able . . .

I would have preferred the second floor, but it is occupied, and so is the first. The three-story buildings in Brumholdstein do not have elevators. You'll have a better view than the couple on the second floor, I was told.

Formerly, on this exact location there had been a rather large camp, built along the lines of a city, with a post office, a library, medical facilities, a bakery, offices, tennis courts, recreation areas, trees, all enclosed by several barbed-wire fences. There were Ger-man signs all over the camp with arrows pointing in one or another direction. The signs are gone, the camp is gone. It no longer exists. Some of the people in Brumholdstein remember playing in that vast camp, by that time completely run down, windows smashed, telephone wires cut, expensive equipment missing, toilets van-dalized. The camp was called Durst. It is not represented in the coloring book. It was built just around the time when Brumhold addressed the student body at the University, attempting to inform them of the plight of their fellow countrymen, Germans who had to leave their homes . . . and the students wept . . . seeing Germans, people like themselves with a bent for meditative thinking, leaving behind what they could not carry with them . . . leaving behind those treasured objects that fall under the philosophical category of: *things*. Tables, chairs, electrical appliances, wood shutters, oak trees, cows, a red barn, a hayfield, all things that in one way or another are reproduced in the coloring book.

Naturally the Durst camp also contained many objects that are to be found on the pages of the coloring book. Benches, chairs, electric light bulbs, kitchen sinks, all now dispersed . . . missing. The familiarity of the objects in the coloring book is reassuring, just as the objects in the Durst camp must have reassured the new arrivals. Ah, look here, a chair, a table. It can't be that bad. And had a coloring book existed of Durst it too would have showed people diligently going about their everyday existence, standing upright, or sitting, or even reclining, chewing food, digesting it, sleeping, walking, all quite normal, speaking before and after breakfast, standing in even rows, saying *Ja* or *Nein* . . . although many, in fact most of the inmates were not German and therefore did not speak a fluent German, which is why most were to some degree deprived in their speech of the proper construction of a German sentence . . . and thus were unable to achieve the level of meditative thinking enjoyed by the average well-educated German student.

Brumhold, who in his works has frequently referred to man's flight from thought, has never found the time to visit the city that was named after him. Admittedly, Brumholdstein is only another display of modern architecture, with nicely designed clusters of residential buildings, and shopping centers with arcades, and conveniently located public toilets marked: *Damen* and *Herren*. By ten in the morning the arcade is crowded with shoppers. But no one appears in any rush. People say: *Bitte* and *Danke*. They do not look at each other suspiciously.

They do not look at me suspiciously. Although I am a foreigner. But they are accustomed to foreigners. They feel quite at ease with foreigners. Particularly with foreigners who are familiar with Bach and with Goethe and with Brumhold . . . All one has to do is mention Brumhold and one is accepted, one might even be called a friend. The Germans are quick to use the word. It may have something to do with their heritage, or the old drinking songs which people still sing . . . In the coloring book it is not too difficult to determine who is who's friend . . . In a sense, everyone depicted in the coloring book is a friend of everyone else.

In 1967 when the first 2,500 apartment units were completed it was decided, on the spur of the moment, that the city should not be named after a statesman, or a poet, or an industrialist, but after a philosopher. Picking the right name was an important event, in part because the city had been built on the site of a former concentration camp. And, in 1967 at least, everyone still felt somewhat disturbed when the subject was raised.

In the great tradition of Greek and German philosophy Brumhold has questioned the meaning, the intrinsic meaning of a *thing* as it manifests itself in the context of metaphysics. There is, moreover, if one stretches the mind a little bit, a certain correlation between a *thing* as we know and understand it to be and 2,500 apartment units, not to mention the additional services, the fire department, post office, library, school, medical facilities, cinema, theater, flower shop, restaurant, coffee shop, bookstore, etc. . . .

Brumhold is by no means a widely read philosopher, but his books are available in Brumholdstein. The Mayor assured me he held Brumhold in great esteem, and so did Wilhelm Aus, the author, whom I visited on my third day in Brumholdstein. Wilhelm Aus being the ostensible reason why I was here.

Knowing something of the history of Brumholdstein, I can only assume that here and there among the population are a number of survivors from the Durst concentration camp. But, for the most part, people here look pretty much alike. Well fed and rather placid. Unless one actually came across a number tattooed on someone's forearm, one could only speculate whether or not the person was a former inmate. Of course, the Germans would be the first to know, the first to recognize a former inmate of Durst.

When Brumhold, like all the men in his age group, was drafted into the militia in 1944, he disconcerted everyone he met by the questions he kept raising regarding the meaning of a *thing* and its correlation to total warfare. If we assume that this is merely a *thing*, he said pointing at his rifle, and this is a *thing*, pointing at his uniform, and each and all of us are doing our *thing*, then our actions, whatever they might be, and whatever they might be called if we were to use the prevailing military terminology, are formulated by our grasp of the *things* around us. Despite the innate grimness of life at that time, Brumhold kept exploring the things he had to do, the things he handled daily in order to implement the things he was ordered to do, although most orders somehow fail to take into consideration the constant narrowing down of certain choices and the elimination of things. Things were being eliminated right and left, in other words, destroyed, put out of action, blown up, erased. Still, as if out of habit, trains kept arriving and departing, trying to meet a certain schedule . . . trying to arrive at a place like Durst, for instance, although each journey entailed a great deal of danger for the men running the train, and the soldiers guarding the train, not to mention the passengers.

The 1940 coloring books are no longer available. They are collector's items by now. Still, indisputably, the things depicted in them are related to the things we find in the latest German coloring book, only the heavy emphasis on the military, on strange salutes, on enthusiastic crowds watching tanks roll by, has been de-emphasized. When Brumhold was drafted into the militia in 1944 there were no coloring books available due to the extreme shortage of paper.

By the time work started on the first 2,500 apartment units, the Durst concentration camp had been almost entirely demolished. In history it took second place to the more notorious camps such as Dachau, Auschwitz, and Treblinka. After giving it some thought, the community decided that the former concentration camp was not worth keeping as a monument. It would not attract a sufficient number of tourists to warrant the extensive repairs that were needed. Furthermore, the camp had only two gas ovens. For the price of rebuilding and maintaining the Durst concentration camp they could build 2,500 apartment units. A lot of kids from the neighboring townships regretted the decision. They used to play soccer and other games on the grounds of the former concentration camp.

The Mayor of Brumholdstein is an affable young man in his thirties. Dark business suit and a polka-dot tie. He introduces me to his wife, and to their friend Ingeborg Platt, a librarian at the local library. I'm afraid we don't carry your books, she said to me.

The Mayor lives in a two-story building that is only a few minutes' walk from the city hall. Three bedrooms, two bathrooms, ping-pong in the basement. Care for a game before dinner, he asks me.

Cold cuts are served at dinner somewhat to my surprise. Smoked sausage, potato salad, crisp green salad, cold beer, then cheese and fruit. I mention how much I liked the design of Brumholdstein.

We're entirely self-sufficient, said the Mayor with a smile. Electrical generator, sewer disposal plant, we even make our own street signs.

Do you have a graveyard, I inquire jokingly.

He frowns. No, not a graveyard. Our population is a young one, although we've had a number of deaths, naturally. At present burials take place in one of the two old graveyards situated in the adjacent county.

Do people ever disappear, I ask.

Disappear? He looks astonished.

In America people frequently disappear. A man or woman goes out to buy a pack of cigarettes or a newspaper and is never seen again.

Why? asked his wife.

They're probably desperate, said Ingeborg Platt.

The Mayor examines me somewhat dubiously. I understand that you will be meeting Wilhelm Aus tomorrow. He is one of our best writers. I hope you will enable him to reach a wider audience.

Are you familiar with his work, I ask Ingeborg Platt.

I find him a bit turgid, and heavy on the politics . . . but he can be fascinating.

He's the new spirit, added the Mayor. A bit to the left, but—

Do you know him well?

The Mayor laughs. Quite well. He is married to my younger

sister. At first he didn't want to move to Brumholdstein. Too modern . . . too antiseptic . . . He was afraid that it would affect his work. But he'll tell you all about it. I'm afraid he's not very reticent . . .

Incidentally, are there any former inmates of the camp living in Brumholdstein?

The Mayor looked blankly at me. Inmates? He turned to his wife. Are there any inmates of the former camp in Brumholdstein? I think, she said slowly, there may be one or two. I think the projectionist at the local cinema is a former inmate . . . someone told me that he was . . .

Some settled in this area, said the Mayor, and became immensely successful. They had a certain advantage.

Advantage?

Well, in having survived, you know.

There are letter boxes on all the streets as well as public telephones. The telephones are not enclosed, and one's conversation could be overheard.

Crime? The Mayor laughs loudly. He is delighted to be questioned about crime. It is virtually nonexistent. Occasionally the police pick up a vagrant, an out-of-towner. They are conspicuous. From the police point of view, he added carefully, Brumholdstein was an easy town to protect. No little alleys, or empty buildings.

I left at ten together with Ingeborg Platt. She was married for five years to an architect. She now lives on the second floor of a red-brick building that is within walking distance of the library. She wears glasses. She too, as a child, used to play on the former grounds of the Durst concentration camp. I discover that she is an avid reader, attends the local performances of the symphony orchestra, and even plays the cello. Her former husband has remarried and lives in Frankfurt. He's an excellent architect, Ingeborg said almost fiercely. He designed the library I work in. The little groups of residential buildings are arranged in such a way as to insure maximum privacy for the tenants of the buildings.

I doubt that anyone saw her visit my apartment. Like the Mayor, she too was born in the neighboring town of Rinz. A great many of her friends still live there.

Why did you really come to Brumholdstein, she asked me.

This is Germany. The doors and windows are different from the ones in America. But they are solid doors and windows. And the people look healthy, self-satisfied, perhaps a shade smug. Not Ingeborg, she's one of the exceptions.

Where were you in 1942.

I wasn't born, answers Ingeborg.

We've just met a few hours ago. We're lying in my bed. Why don't you remove your shirt, she asks. We only know each other for five or six hours. Do take off your shirt, she says. She is naked and crouching on the floor in front of me. Actually, she is not crouching on the bare floor, but on a carpet that was manufactured in Germany. She knows the Mayor and his family, Wilhelm Aus and his family, and the bookseller Sonk who is a bachelor. She sees them all quite frequently. I watch her crouching in front of me. Who else, I wonder, shares this vision of Ingeborg with me?

Ingeborg is attempting to give me pleasure. She is doing it in a completely selfless and unselfconscious manner. It is, admittedly, not an entirely new experience, but the familiarity of the experience is colored by the unfamiliar world around me, a world housing unfamiliar *things*, that the remoteness, the polite distance between Ingeborg and myself serves only to intensify, although what I interpret as distance may merely be due to the way we express or fail to express ourselves in both English and German.

So when she asked: Was that nice? I didn't really know if it was . . . being annoyed by the way the question was phrased, being irritated by the word nice, being reluctant to say yes, not because the experience had not been *nice* but because the word nice had been discarded long ago from my day-to-day vocabulary.

I will have them order all your books at the library, she said later, trying to please me.
That's nice.

Ingeborg's father had been a colonel in the Waffen SS. I showed her my coloring book and the crayons. Surprised by her response, forcibly having to restrain her from coloring the pages. It is a gift for a little boy, I said.

Is your father alive, I asked her cautiously.
Oh yes, he's just retired.
From the army?
Oh no, from a bank . . .

Shortly before she left, she said: Well, another German experience for you . . . and because she was speaking in English, I couldn't determine the degree to which she intended this statement to be an accusation.

The people of Rinz, a neighboring town where Ingeborg grew up, had grave reservations regarding the building of a city so near their town. Brumholdstein, once completed, would attract people from all over Germany. There would be more cars, more roads, more bars, more stores, more single people, more venereal disease, more crime, more fires, more schools, more police, and higher taxes and an end to the tranquility they had enjoyed for so many years . . .

At night I feel somewhat chilly and cover myself with another blanket that had been thoughtfully provided for me. The local German newspaper is delivered to my door. Among other details it also lists the daily TV programs. Glancing at the listing I discover that Wilhelm Aus is to be interviewed the following day at 10 a.m.

I came to Brumholdstein in order to visit Wilhelm Aus. He is expecting me. And quite clearly, to judge from the TV interview, he's an old hand at being interviewed. Born in 1946, he has published three novels, and two books of essays. He is referred to as one of the young and upcoming German writers. As a child he played in the Durst concentration camp with his school friends. Although not exactly unaware of the purpose the camp had served during the war, he and his friends in converting sections of the camp to another purpose saw no reason ever to dwell on what may or may not have taken place in the large shower room where they played handball, or on the parade ground where they played soccer . . . Much to Wilhelm's regret, he did not excel at any sport. He did not excel at anything. No one, not even his teachers, had any inkling that he would become an influential writer. Even his parents were surprised. Gradually they came to accept his decision to become a writer, just as they had come to accept his left-wing politics. Mr. Wilhelm Aus cuts his own hair, which is why the local barber looks at me with blank eyes when I mention Aus. *Aus, Aus? Nein, denn kenn ich nicht.*

Ingeborg had asked me if I was married.
Yes, I said.
What is she like?
I showed her a photograph I carry in my wallet.
She's attractive . . . what does she do?
She's a psychologist. As a matter of fact, she also happens to be Jewish, and a number of her close relatives were killed in the Durst concentration camp.
Seeing the startled look on Ingeborg's face, I burst out laughing. No . . . no . . . forgive me, I couldn't resist saying that . . .
Saying what? That your wife is a psychologist, that she is Jewish, or that her relatives were killed in Durst.
The last bit about her relatives. I don't know where they were killed. Forgive me, it was a terribly cruel thing to say to you.
I take it that she didn't wish to accompany you to Germany, said Ingeborg.
Not exactly. In a manner of speaking we are separated . . .
Divorced?
No . . . living apart.
I see. She has her life and you have yours.

Did this conversation really take place? Can I rely on my memory? The people in the coloring book go about their daily business, and in doing so they too have to rely on their memory. Anything in the world can trigger a recollection of an event. Ingeborg left her scarf in my apartment. She forgot it. It is a bright-colored silk scarf made in India. It has been left behind to remind me of an event that had taken place in this third-floor apartment.

It goes without saying that a large number of people in Brumholdstein are aware of my presence.

What is he doing in Brumholdstein?
He came to interview Wilhelm Aus.
What is he doing now?
He is watching TV.
What did he do last night?
He made love to Ingeborg Platt.
Why didn't he remove his shirt?

Well, Ingeborg, says Wilhelm. I hear you've gone to bed with our visitor from America.
One can't any longer keep any secrets, she replies.
He's married, I take it.
Yes . . . but they're separated. He hasn't seen her in some time.
Why did he refuse to take off his shirt?
Because he is hiding something.
What could he be hiding beneath his shirt?

During the TV interview Wilhelm Aus refers to the foreign laborers in Germany. Our garbage is being hauled away by Turks, Yugoslavs, and Italians, our streets are being cleaned by Rumanians. These people are providing us with cheap labor. We are exploiting them.

Wilhelm Aus is married to an attractive blonde schoolteacher. They have three children. Each year they take their vacation in the Black Forest where they rent a large cottage. They eat sausage three times a week. It is my impression that neither Wilhelm or his wife appear likely to do anything unexpected . . . commit suicide, disappear, or kill someone . . . It is just an impression. I have been proved incorrect once before. There are white tiles on the floor of their apartment. The metal railing on the staircase is black. The stairs like the exterior of the building are also made of red brick. There are two apartments on each floor, although now and then a more affluent family occupies an entire floor.

Mr. and Mrs. Wilhelm Aus are not affluent. There are three children to be fed. In twenty years, provided nothing unexpected takes place, they may become affluent and occupy the next-door apartment. Naturally, Wilhelm Aus may just strike it lucky with one of his novels one day. But this seems, given the experimental nature of his work, somewhat unlikely. In the TV interview the likelihood of his occupying the next-door apartment is not mentioned. It is not controversial enough. It does not have sufficient public appeal, besides it may alarm his next-door neighbor.

On my second visit Mr. Aus says, call me Wilhelm. His wife says, call me Johanna.

Wilhelm Aus accompanies me back to my place. In the evening he walks his dog. They stop periodically at a street lamp, a post box, a public telephone, a parked car. Each evening they follow the same route. Each evening Wilhelm Aus meditatively watches the yellow stream of his dog's urine stain the sidewalk, or the tire of a German car. What is Wilhelm thinking as he watches his dog piss? He knows that I have slept with his friend Ingeborg. Both he and his wife know that I have failed to undress completely while making love to their close friend. Why don't you take off your shirt, Ingeborg had asked. I prefer not to, I replied.

The bookstore is on the main street. The owner, Max Sonk, a former student of philosophy, had studied with Brumhold in 1941 and 1942.

On his desk there's a photograph of Brumhold addressing the student body of Mannheim University in 1936. The photograph is inscribed to, My dear Max Sonk. Max Sonk knows who I am, but he is outwardly, at least, indifferent to my presence in his bookstore. He sees Ingeborg at least twice a week. Like me he has been to bed with her.

Mr. Sonk congratulates Wilhelm Aus on the telephone for the way he handled the interview on TV. You were really excellent. I admire your candor.
   Have you seen Ingeborg lately, Wilhelm Aus wants to know.
   We've had a slight falling out. She'll probably come around in a day or two.

Now the street signs and all the directional signs that are erected on the highway are being manufactured in Brumholdstein. Once they were made in the neighboring town. It goes without saying that the people of Rinz deeply resent this. They also resent that the few foreigners employed by the department of public works in Brumholdstein all live in Rinz. Now we have Turks and Rumanians walking on our streets, is the common complaint. Despite everything that is being said about them, the Italians, Turks, and Yugoslavs are hard workers. The streets of Brumholdstein are clean, the garbage is picked up on time. No complaints there. But no one really wishes to have these people as next-door neighbors. As neighbors they leave a lot to be desired. In no time little grocery stores carrying foreign foods are opening up on every corner in Rinz.

I took Ingeborg to a Chinese restaurant . . .
Why do you dislike me so much, she asked.
Are you quite sure you have the right person, I answered.

In the coloring book there is no evidence of anyone ever showing any dislike for another person or thing. Dislike has been permanently effaced from the world of this coloring book. The faces still awaiting to receive their color show only contentment and pleasure.

Is everything satisfactory? asked the Chinese waiter.

But why did you pick on me? Ingeborg asked.
I don't really understand what you're saying.

At night I feel chilly and get up for another blanket. I am by now accustomed to sleeping alone. After a week in Brumholdstein, I've come to feel at home in this apartment. There's a white telephone at my bedside in case I wish to make a call at night, or receive one. There is another phone in the kitchen, also white, and a third, this one is black, in the living room, just to make sure that I won't miss a call. In the living room on a shelf there are a number of German and English books. Among the German books are two by Brumhold, *Ja oder Nein* and his great classic, *Uber die Bewegung aller Dinge.*

Before going to bed a man takes a shower, brushes his teeth. So far, nothing unusual. Like most people, whatever I do inside the bathroom is done unthinkingly. In a sense, all my needs are being

taken care of. They have even provided me with a typewriter.
The refrigerator is stocked. More cold cuts and beer.

This city is named after a German philosopher, who, like so many
of his predecessors, inquired into the nature of a *thing*. He started
his philosophical inquiry by simply asking: *What is a thing?* For
most of the inhabitants of Brumholdstein the question does not
pose a great problem. They are the first to acknowledge that the
hot and cold water taps in the bathroom are things, just as much
as the windows in the new shopping center are things. Things
pervade every encounter, every action. In that respect, the person
who says, I'm doing my thing, may have a construction of per-
sonal events in mind, the self receiving a priority over the things
without which the self could never even formulate a conception
of its role.

Are you married? asked Johanna.
Yes.
You should have brought your wife along.
She was here in Germany a long time ago.
Wilhelm did not ask me when.
What does she do? asked his wife.
She's a psychoanalyst.
How fascinating.
That could be a problem, said Wilhelm slyly.
Not any more, I explained.
They looked inquiringly at me.
Initially it was something of a problem, but not any more . . .

I wash my hands. The desk is uncluttered. I find a ream of paper
in one of the drawers. In another drawer there's a German-English
dictionary, a bottle of Pelikan fountain pen ink, an eraser, a plastic
ruler, and a small stapler.

I look up the German word for missing. It is *abwesend*, or *fehlend*,
or *nicht zu finden*. I also look up the word, disappear. It is
verschwinden.

I telephone Ingeborg, wishing to apologize for my rudeness the
night before. But no one answers. Finally I leave the apartment.
The tobacconist from whom I buy a pack of cigarettes used to

live in Berlin. On an impulse I buy a lottery ticket although I don't expect to be in Germany when the winners of the lottery are announced. I ask the young waitress at the small restaurant where I have a late breakfast if she was born in the area. She laughs. Oh yes. Did you also come here to play before they started to build Brumholdstein. Oh yes, we all did. At first the guards who guarded the empty camp used to chase us away . . . but after a while they became less strict about it. The short stout man at the next table is listening to our conversation. He is holding a newspaper in front of him, while eating scrambled eggs, fried potatoes, and sausage . . .

After a careful search that afternoon I found the old railroad tracks. They run parallel to the main highway. There was very little traffic at that hour. I parked my car on the side of the highway and followed the tracks on foot for a mile or so. No one saw me. I encountered no one. In the distance I could make out the taller buildings of Brumholdstein. On a siding I passed an old railroad freight car. Its sliding doors wide open. It was a German freight car. For no reason in particular I scratched a long row of numbers on its side.

Miss Ingeborg Platt failed to show up at the library on Monday morning. She usually arrived at nine-thirty. She would take her one-hour break at twelve. In the past she had always called in when, for one reason or another, she couldn't come to work that day. She liked her job and was exceptionally good at it. For the past two years she had been in charge of cataloguing. Although somewhat remote, she was well liked by the staff. She was neat, methodical, accurate, with an excellent memory for the titles and names of authors of the books she catalogued, and the dates of their arrival at the library. It so happened that she also happened to be an avid reader, quite eclectic in her taste, reading anything that stimulated her imagination. She was able to borrow books before they were put into circulation. That has long been one of the few privileges librarians possess. Although well liked she had few friends.

Was she really well liked, I asked Wilhelm, after she had been missing for a few days. No, she was not. She kept herself apart from the others. I think she was afraid of being rejected. She was also afraid that they might find out that her father had been the former commander of the Durst concentration camp, although, I should think, that is common knowledge by now.

She told me that the last time I saw her, I admitted.
And?
And nothing.

When she failed to show up at work, the chief librarian, a Mr. Runz, concerned that she might not be feeling well, telephoned her several times during the day. Receiving no reply, he drove over to where she lives at around five-thirty. After trying her doorbell a number of times, he went to see the superintendent, a Mr. Kurtz, who was most reluctant to become involved. Only after a great deal of persuasion did Mr. Kurtz open her apartment door. The place was empty. Nothing seemed to be missing. It was Mr. Kurtz who noticed that the electric plug of the refrigerator had been pulled out of the socket in the wall. The refrigerator was stocked with food, cold cuts, vegetables, meat, milk, butter, beer . . .

Wilhelm rang me late at night to tell me that Ingeborg was missing. He called to inquire if by any chance I had seen her that day. I suppose it was a tactful way of trying to discover if she was staying with me.
   I haven't seen her since last Thursday. We had dinner together at the Chinese restaurant. She seemed quite cheerful at the time.
   What did she wear?
   An ivory-colored dress with gold buttons.
   I'll come to see you tomorrow, said Wilhelm. He sounded cold and stiff.

This being Germany, a nation known for its thoroughness, I expected to be questioned by the police. But they never got in touch with me. The Mayor called me the next day, and awkwardly made up some excuse as to why he couldn't see me at his home that evening. I never called him to say good-by.

I did not object when Wilhelm came by to take me to Ingeborg's apartment. He simply said I might help him determine if something was missing. I had spent two nights and several evenings at her place, and by now was quite familiar with the layout. I could see it with my eyes shut. It was forever imprinted on my mind. White walls. A bedroom, a living room, a small kitchen. Room enough for one or two people, and their objects, their things. There were plants, a stereo, books, a few drawings on the wall. Her suitcases were in one of the two built-in closets. The ivory-colored dress was hanging in the other closet. There were no notes. Her check book, bank book, and other personal papers were in a drawer of her desk. Wilhelm came across the coloring book I had given her. He did not object when I took it with me. He didn't seem to care very much about it. I also pocketed the crayons.

Wilhelm told me that he had been in touch with her former husband.

What about her parents?

They haven't been on speaking terms for years.

Why did she disappear, I asked.

Evidently something must have happened, said Wilhelm grimly.

Whatever it was, it could have been troubling her for a long time.

Yes, Wilhelm agreed. But it also could have happened just now.

She'll be back, I said without much conviction.

I doubt it, replied Wilhelm.

Going through her desk drawers I came across a photo of a group of skeletons like men standing in a row, posing for the photographer. Wilhelm studied the photograph, the building in the rear was one of the buildings in the former Durst concentration camp. The men were smiling incongruously. They were leaning against each other for support. Under a magnifying glass I could clearly make out the numbers tattooed on their forearms.

This photo must have been taken a day or two after the camp was liberated by the Americans, said Wilhelm. I made absolutely no move to stop him as he carefully and deliberately tore the photo into tiny shreds. I did not lift a hand to stop him from effacing the past.

When I left Brumholdstein, no one saw me off.

I had a cup of coffee at the airport snack bar. The short stocky man at the next table raised a stein of beer. *Prost,* I said. Just before takeoff, I tossed the coloring book and the crayons into a garbage can. The man who stamped my passport said: Come back soon.

Auf wiedersehen.

AUTHOR'S NOTE: *A passage in "The New Spirit," a prose poem by John Ashbery, led me to write "The English Garden." The title of my story is also taken from the same passage, which appears on page 27 of his book,* Three Poems, *published by Viking Press in 1972.*—W. A.

O MY GENERATION

ARAM SAROYAN

I

O my generation
        Faster than a speeding bullet
        More like the blinking of an eye
        Or a shadow on the grass
        Ah, the dark clouds, the rain
        Followed by the sun in bloom

O my generation
        A bowl of Corn Flakes, Rice Krispies
        Or on cold mornings Cream of Wheat
        Innocent in our school clothes
        America in Korea, numbers and letters
        How do I write my name?

O my generation
        The softness of a spring breeze
        The ease of birds singing in daylight
        A cowboy picture on TV, a cowboy outfit
        To get all dressed up in, chaps & spurs
        To make another meaning of oneself

O my generation
     We were so young and innocent
     Just like children, just like children always
     And then came the locomotive
     And then came mathematics
     And then came the endless chatter

O my generation
     With a magnifying glass and a gum wrapper
     With a piece of paper and a comb
     With a bicycle, some playing cards, and clothespins
     With a slingshot, a bow & arrow, a bb-gun
     O my generation, with pick-up-sticks

O my generation
     With windows & doors, and patios
     Swimming pools and gymnasiums
     I.D. bracelets and comic books
     O my generation and movie magazines
     Confidential, Police Gazette, Gypsy Rose Lee

O my generation
     And bus stops, shoe-shine parlors
     Movie houses and nightmares
     O my generation and Mr. Sandman
     Tea for Two, Martin and Lewis, Perry Como
     O my generation and The Hit Parade

O my generation
     And Debbie & Eddie, and Bob & Natalie
     I Like Ike buttons, alleys and boredom
     O my generation and Dragnet
     Black and white television, hopeless cases
     A deck of playing cards & Marilyn Monroe

O my generation
     Flying a kite, riding a bicycle
     Watching the light fail as we played before dinner
     O my generation and the promise of love
     A beautiful girl from school on the elevator
     Headlocks and hammerlocks, ducktails and pants real low

O my generation
>   Fist fights, and feel-ups, neckties and report cards
>   O my generation and strange teachers
>   O my generation and being sent to the principal's office
>   Full of terror, full of stories
>   And the principal one more harassed man only

O my generation
>   And the strange smell of other people's houses
>   A feeling like falling off the world
>   O my generation and first shy friendships
>   Indian wrestling, playing catch
>   O my generation and the Soap Box Derby

O my generation
>   We grow up so fast, and yet we don't know
>   O my generation in locker rooms and coffee shops
>   And walking downtown and uptown
>   And o my generation and sincerity
>   And beauty, and truth, sex and love

II

O my generation
>   We were just barely out of the gate
>   We were hardly out of the nest
>   We were still children really
>   We didn't know what hit us
>   We were like totally innocent

O my generation
>   Smoking marijuana and not even getting high
>   O my generation, finally getting high
>   Everything definite and funny, cracking up laughing
>   While reading the menu, the range of choices and prices
>   Cosmically disorienting, I'll have pea soup

O my generation
  A snowstorm of speed, a shot in the bathroom
  And a rearranged living room, who was that guy
  Anyway, o my generation, time melting in rooms
  All over America while Vietnam exploded
  O my generation the grammar the syntax gone

O my generation
  Our eyes too open, too vulnerable, too full of chemicals
  O my generation and white bread, hamburgers
  O my generation and butter
  O my generation and thoughts of success
  O my generation and long hair

O my generation
  Our membership in glances, our innocent reward
  O my generation at midnight at Winterland
  At the Fillmore, at Max's Kansas City
  O my generation and Dylan, the Shakespeare of the Sixties
  O my generation and Andy, the Rembrandt of Now

O my generation
  And Allen Ginsberg, weeping on the Lower East Side
  And Gary Snyder, honing his craft in a monastery
  And Philip Whalen, a jolly Buddha
  And Jack Kerouac, with a red neck to disguise
  His own difficult rainbow

O my generation
  With Jimi and Janis and Jim Morrison
  So quickly they were gone
  Leaving us the open book of their lives
  If we could read between the lines
  And the music like red, green, yellow, and blue

O my generation
  A piece of soot in our eye
  Our brains soft with time departed into
  Bright rooms of incense, dim rooms of incense
  A retinal circus on the subway
  A whole lifetime in the way a man walks

O my generation
        With all the doors open
        O my generation with the windows lifted wide
        O my generation with a whole new system
        O my generation with our arms spread too wide
        O my generation ready for evil

O my generation
        Then the evil did arrive
        O my generation and Lancelot and Groovey on the Lower
            East Side
        O my generation and The Chicago Convention of Life
            spilling its blood
        O my generation and Manson's caravan demonstrating for
            Evil like a Washington lobby
        O my generation and the other look in our eye

O my generation
        And the strangeness and the fright
        O my generation and a different way of life
        O my generation back on the drawing board
        O my generation sick at heart, and body, and mind
        O my generation looking for a new way out

O my generation
        Going off by itself, without farewell
        O my generation feeling like a bit of fresh air
        O my generation reading a book for the first time in years
        O my generation suddenly, silently crying
        O my generation with a gentle hand on its own face

III

O my generation
        We were too young for the Beats
        Not quite young enough for the Flower Powers
        We were adolescents wth Hemingway and Fitzgerald
        Adults with Abbie and Jerry
        But not quite any of them

O my generation
    We were too quickly ourselves
    Not to be casualties of the blind spots in our make-ups
    O my generation and Women's Liberation
    O my generation and getting married
    O my generation and natural childbirth

O my generation
    A little baby is an awesome event
    O my generation a new kind of experience
    Every minute taken up, no time for conflict
    O my generation turning the corner of life
    O my generation a mother and a father

O my generation
    It happened so fast
    We weren't ready for this, we couldn't do it together
    O my generation and single mothers and
    Single fathers, the children hauling us
    Back into time, pushing space aside

O my generation
    A child's first words, uttered with all its nervous system
    O my generation remembering itself so young
    O my generation with sudden sympathy for our parents
    O my generation doing a difficult job
    O my generation trying to find clean air for the child
        to breathe

O my generation
    And Welfare, because if you have a child and no money
        you qualify
    O my generation a better way of life every first of
        the month
    O my generation and food stamps, three big boxes at the
        Co-op, all organic
    O my generation gardening
    O my generation fixing a hole in the roof

O my generation
>   And Jesus, and the I Ching, and the stars at night
>   O my generation and a rooster at dawn
>   O my generation and the old-timers, with years of
>   experience in their voices
>   O my generation and admiration for the simple people,
>   the survivors
>   O my generation and flowers in the house

O my generation
>   And silence at the end of the day
>   And the body tired out from the hundred stops and starts
>   O my generation and the phases of the moon
>   O my generation and neighbors
>   O my generation and exercise and diet

O my generation
>   The trees are forever in motion, rooted in the earth
>   The rain comes down and waters the plants
>   And then evaporates into the air again through the leaves
>   O my generation and spring water, rain water, well water,
>   water from the creek
>   O my generation the night air so fine

O my generation
>   The time almost disappeared
>   We shortened our names and let our hair grow
>   We knew each other by our clothes
>   But we couldn't live for long inside that perfect dream
>   Our life kept interrupting us with truth

O my generation
>   We are going home into the numbers of the earth
>   We have arrived again in minutes, and hours
>   Days and weeks, months and years
>   Time couldn't forget us, even in the Eternal Present
>   We are arriving back into life

O my generation
>It's time to hold on with all our mights
>But it may be easier than we think
>After all, this is the way it goes
>A child blows a bubble and asks you to come and see
>And the cat is also hungry

NGHSI-ALTAI

An excerpt from the novel *Daily Lives in Nghsi-Altai*

ROBERT NICHOLS

After traveling in the country for a year we have this brief history of the place out of the mouth of a shaman. The Blue Shamans are but one of the several societies of men here. Therefore we cannot vouch for its authenticity.

In any case the mythological origins are barely worth recording.

Prehistory: Forest covered the world, according to old legend. It was the era of the so-called "Walking Trees." For a long time the trees with their dense tops were able to keep out Sky, so the story goes. One day the trees weakened. Sky punched a hole in and entered accompanied by her brother, a monkey called Weather.

The southern half of the world was flooded and drowned in lakes. The north half received no water at all; it became dry steppe. The sun turned all the steppe dwellers (men, ostriches, goats, and camels) as brown as dung. The rain falling in twilight turned the skin of the forest dwellers blue as lichen.

A wall was built between the Wet and the Dry by Monkey, which he called "The Divider." All elements of the world were separated: the Sky, Earth, and Forest, the wet sacred men and the dry men. They conspired to punish Monkey. The wall was thrown down into a ditch, the present Rift Canyon, and the Karsts (Monkey's descendants) were given no skin color at all: they are albinos.

From the "three skins" and the "three weathers" (or types of environment) the fields of knowledge are supposed to have been elaborated: agriculture, the ecological sciences, and trade.

Possible archeological periods (prehistory) suggested by the above.

FOREST—mezazoic stone-age culture. Wandering hunters and food gatherers.

LAKE—neolithic. The beginning of settled culture, the villages.

PLAINS—early bronze age. Subduing of the country by pastoral nomads.

FROM THE 1st THROUGH 4th MILLENNIUM/A Plains Tribal Culture

This period begins with neolithic village culture already established.

Grave diggings deep under the loessal soil show that there were three tribes living in the plains simultaneously. Archaeologists call these the "gray pottery" people—Yang Shao. The "black pottery" people—Lung Shan. And the "painted pottery" people: the Jats.

The Jats appear to have migrated from northern India via the Khyber Pass through Turkestan and Iran, where they learned bronze age techniques: metal-smithing, the wheel (for chariots), and writing. From the plateau they migrated eastward, a ferocious cavalry, across the desert, hopping from one oasis to the next and intermarrying with the local folk.

However, they finally reached the plains in a state of exhaustion, not as conquerors but as a conquered people. They were absorbed in part by the other two tribes, and the bronze age discoveries appear to have been suppressed during the first millennium. (Bronze war axes have been found in the graves buried *below* neolithic pottery.)

This is the period of village high culture (neolithic). From a number of epicenters the population spread through the plains. The pattern of movement operated in this way:

First there was the "mother village": a hundred or so pit dwellings surrounding a long house. This was attached to a cemetery presided over by the shaman (ancestor worship). All the great neolithic discoveries are in evidence here: house-building (posts with wattle-and-daub construction), pottery molds and kilns, spindle whorls and needles, stone polishers, the tools of agriculture, and the bones of domesticated animals: the dog, the sheep, pigs, horses, and cattle. There were also extensive cattle herds and the beginnings of rice agriculture.

This improved food supply increased the number of inhabitants in the "mother village." Several "daughter villages" would be established, still using the same cemetery and under the authority of the original priesthood. In this way the plains were populated.

High village culture seems to have prevailed during the first three millennia—the settlements in much the same form as they are today. However, at the end of the 3rd millennium there was a decline.

Bad agricultural practices. Overgrazing by cattle, the plowing of unsuitable land for crops, and a prolonged drought brought an end to this early period. Much of the plains became dust bowl. Productivity declined in the pasture lands. The burning of cow dung for fuel removed it from reuse on the fields as fertilizer. On the little arable land that remained the crop rotation system was abandoned.

Destruction of the irrigation system by rabbits.

Starvation threatened, with a rising population now divided into rich and poor. Under pressure of population the regular food chain was broken. It was no longer plant (grains and legumes) → to animal (protein) → to Man, the original sequence. But simplified to the direct chain: plant → to human. The property owners ate only black millet, while the tenants and a landless proletariat subsisted on rice gruel and during famine grubbed for roots.

Fortunately this period ended with the discovery by Jats of fossil fuel. A fragment of "painted pottery" of the 4th millennium depicts what seems to have been a natural gas strike. With the development of this substitute fuel (that is, substitute for cow dung) it was possible to reverse the above cycle and restore productivity. The Jats also developed a primitive textile industry using synthetic fibers.

Thus they gained an advantage over the other plains tribes. Gradual extension of Jat hegemony in the latter half of the 4th millennium. Main features of the present-day culture are established; that is, the matriarchy, limited polygyny and village exogamous marriage, conservative economic planning, and government under the panchayat system.

Present calendar of holidays is set. Inauguration of the Great Festivals.

4th THROUGH 5th MILLENNIUM/A Karst Commercial Empire

It is thought that the Karsts were originally lake dwellers. With geological transformation of the plateau, desiccation due to weather changes, and the gradual subsidence of the great Rift Valley, the area became the present "dry beds." The tribe continued to live there, inhabiting the beaks and dolomitic caves. From cave dwellers they became miners, excavating the subsurface for minerals. This was the source of their wealth.

The Karsts are a naturally egalitarian people, with a strong aptitude for mechanics. A corporation of free citizens developed the mines. Special machinery was adapted for digging, and for ventilating and pumping water. Through pumps the properties of air (also a vacuum) were discovered. This led rapidly to the discovery of other gases, and laid the foundation for their future chemical industry.

Thus, hydraulics led to science, science to trade, and trade to the evolution of money and a competitive market system. Domination of the other territories followed. The earlier portion of the 5th millennium was the great trading period of the Karsts, with their merchants spreading over the plains and Drunes, or forest regions. The great city-based merchant houses joined with the local overlords in a profitable alliance. Usually one of the members of a Jat family was assigned to handle the Karsts' commercial affairs. These enterprising young men often became tax collectors.

The Rift Canyon was now completely urbanized. As trade developed there was further rationalization of industry, particularly metals and chemicals. With the spread of the industrial corporation and further capital accumulation, finally the entire Rift had been organized into a national industrial system centered upon the steel industry. The government was one of nominal parliamentary democracy, with two parties. One of these, the Managers, were in firm control. Opposed to them was a weak Decentralist party.

Certain tendencies, however, favored the Decentralists. One of these was the rigidity of the economic system itself. Its very success hampered it. Inventions were held off the market by the monopolists. There was little adaptation of machines to changing circumstances, due to heavy capitalization and vested marketing arrangements. Ingenuity flagged. In its partnership with business the State subsidized an inflated "public sector" which absorbed unemployables and bankrupt industries. However, this resulted in increased inefficiency and inflation. A large advertising and transportation sector, once a stimulus, now became a drag on the economy. Agriculture was depressed.

Opposed to all this, the Decentralists stood for flexibility and free application of current inventions, and also for the freeing of the satellite "countryside" from the metropolis.

At this juncture, there appeared on the scene two inventions of especial consequence: one was the small and compact hydrogen furnace, to substitute for the huge blast furnace of the classical steel industry, and along with it the small planetary mill, to replace the long steel rolling mill. At the same time, certain new processes (called "pugging") made it economical to work outlying low-grade ore deposits in the plains. This was done by certain native capitalists (Jats)—who became convinced Decentralists. Advances in computerization and microcircuitry also favored small units. Thus, it became possible to have a regionally based, rather than national, metals industry. All these methods were outlawed by the Managers.

A black market developed, in which there was extensive bootlegging of the new techniques. Capitalist groups in the plains were soon to organize the machinery banks. They were allied with workers of certain Karst industries, who were beginning to call themselves "syndicalists" or "anarchosyndicalists."

A split developed among the Decentralists—a part of whom became the "Decembrists." This faction wanted to go underground and develop "subregions." Their slogan was "Every village its own steel mill" and "Factories in the caves." However, they did not arm for fear of provoking State repressions. The other side pushed for a parliamentary solution. A revived Decentralist party won the next parliamentary contest and swept the elections.

They had not reckoned on the perfidy of the Managers. A counterrevolutionary coup soon followed. All the Decentralist officials (representing a majority of the people) were either killed or exiled.

The Managers were more firmly in control than ever. By now they had adopted many of the technical innovations promoted by the Decentralists and absorbed the best ideas of the opposition. Thus, under the slogan: "Abolish the State," the State was able to perpetuate itself for a thousand years.

At the end of the 4th millenium there was a civil war in which the State fell and was replaced by authentic popular institutions.

These are the urban factory "syndicates" and the farm collectives (run jointly with the machine banks) that survive to this day.

Golden age of the popular Decentralists.

6th MILLENIUM TO THE PRESENT/The Explosion of a Theocracy

The original Thays and Deodars lived in the forest undisturbed. The Thays are a slight, fair-skinned people probably of Indonesian origin. The stately and blue-skinned Deodars are of Tibetan stock, deeply mystical practitioners of a nature animism. From the beginning the two peoples lived together amicably in the forest under a confederacy of tribes or "gentes." They were hunters and herb gatherers. The Deodars, in particular, were skilled in medicine. An early woodland Deodar, Orpheo, is supposed to have invented music, while listening to the sighing of boughs.

At the dawn of historical time the confederacy had no center, merely shifted in the woods. Its members practiced "swidden agriculture," that is slash and burn: planting their seeds in a clearing made by stone axes, then moving on. Their shelters were of bamboo and leaves caked with mud—pitched in places selected by the shamans.

With the penetration of the Drunes by the Karsts in the middle of the 3rd millennium, the confederacy dissolved. There was intense trade exploitation. The forest sellers widened their clearings to trade tea, tung oil, and indigo, also skins and the feathers of birds, in exchange for trinkets from the Karsts and metals. They also took up basket-weaving for cash.

As there was a limit to the size of clearings but not to rising productivity of the Karsts whose manufactured products increased each year, the foresters ran into debt. They were also divided among themselves. The basket-makers became enriched. Gradually the consumption of luxury goods from the Rift gave rise to a privileged class of traders, landowners and moneylenders.

This led to more intense exploitation of the Drunes, in particular the establishment of native manufactures, including a large plywood industry using the poorer Thays as captive labor. The Thay tribes became completely colonized by the Karsts, and today speak only the Karst language.

The Deodars retreated further into the woods. Meanwhile their shamans had become smiths. They set up forges in the deep woods, operated by skin bellows decorated with feathers; there they worked the metal traded from the Karsts. They learned how to draw wire: copper, for which there was only an ornamental use at this time, for jewelry; and steel wire which replaced catgut for musical instrument strings.

It was at this time among the Deodars that the forest universities began. They had originally been hospitals. Diseases had infected the Drunes from the Rift, among the most serious being syphilis. For some reason the highest incidence of this was among the former shamans. The disease was cured by herbal medicine. It has been said the practice of celibacy among the Drune priesthood originated at this time. In any case a religious revival transformed the hospitals into monasteries. From monasteries they became universities.

It was natural that the first studies were of forestry, natural history, and public medicine—which were to become later the nuclei of the ecological sciences. Trees were planted; the forest recovered the lower slopes. The first environmental testing devices were originated in the Drunes. Using their medical knowledge and their resonating wires, instruments of all kinds were elaborated, which gave precise ratios and measured the most minute differences among natural phenomena. There were also advanced studies of insects.

When communication was later reopened with the rest of the country, knowledge of these Deodar sciences spread throughout the plains and dry beds. This period saw also the hiring of the first sensors—to man testing laboratories associated with the early machinery banks and factory syndicates.

Toward the end of the 6th millennium there was renewed trouble in the Rift. The Decentralist technology had been consolidated after the civil war, and the anarchosyndicalist political system was both efficient and relatively humane. But the economy was overproductive. Intensive development led to depletion of the natural resources of the country; the riches of the soil and subsoil were squandered in an orgy of materialist consumption. The crops of monoagriculture were ravaged by bugs, despite inspection stations at every border. At the same time water and atmospheric pollution increased. This was due primarily to the Jat gas engine—which though a benefit to the sparsely populated early communes had become a disaster in an age of overpopulation. With overdevelopment and wasting of resources came unemployment, and with unemployment, poverty. There was general social unrest and violence; and the regional governments, which had originally been libertarian, grew increasingly harsh and repressive. Persecutions of students and intellectuals followed, and these fled to the Drunes.

It is not surprising that the next period, which has lasted about 400 years from the end of the 6th millennium, has been the most fruitful in Deodar history. It has been marked by two main developments: an intensive effort to extend theoretical ecology to regulate actual economic production throughout the country, and a radical transformation of the Deodar priesthood.

This latter point requires explanation. During the previous millennium the priesthood had been in the main otherworldly and quietist. It had been also corrupt. But it was revived by the persecutions. At the onset of the environmental crisis in the plains and dry beds, political dissenters were granted asylum by the Deodars. With the worsening of the crisis, the regional police—organized into companies of "berserks"—actually pursued the dissenters into the Drunes, and in the end the Drunes was invaded and occupied completely. The Deodar priesthood committed by religion to nonviolence could now not help but put that doctrine into practice: total nonresistance to force, at the same time total noncooperation was followed. Orders given by the conquerors were received but never carried out, and the invading bands were at first neutralized and later completely absorbed—not without a number of martyrdoms on the part of Deodar High Officials. The theocracy was decimated—and transformed.

The country was now divided into two worlds. In both the environment was equally threatened. This challenge was tackled directly—principally by the scientist-exiles (from the plains and Rift) now associated with the Drune universities. A new conservation and resource technology came into being, directed toward maintaining population and resources in dynamic balance in what came to be called the "open steady state planning." For this a new "embryology computer" became a chief instrument. In technology, pollutants and combustive fuels were outlawed and alternative solar and wind energy systems developed, along with the first waste recycling industries.

Religion revived based on the "Six Tendencies" which—now

nourished by science—had survived from the ancient animism. Elsewhere in the country the authority of the old production managers had declined, and that of the sensors attached to the weather and soils stations was strengthened. These young Drune sensors had migrated in ever-increasing numbers into the Rift and plains. With the worsening of the ecological crisis, the sensor stations tended to take on some of the extra functions of the local administration, and to absorb some of the productive features of the panchayats. Thus, what came to be called the "Blue Revolution" radiated outward from its twin centers: the forest exiles and sensors.

At this juncture a decisive and quite fortuitous event tipped the balance: the discovery of electricity in one of the forest universities by a Drune named Mazdo. This discovery was quickly applied, and grafted onto the new solar and wind technology, bringing practical benefits to each town and village and immeasurably adding to the power of the conservationists. New windmills produced electricity; and sun, which had before merely produced heat, generated a whole spectrum of photochemical energies.

Thus, under its double slogan, "Electrification/Conservation" and "Blue World," the scientific revolution was achieved, and the confederacy of Nghsi-Altai established in its present outline.

HORSES BEFORE TROY

MELIH CEVDET ANDAY

Translated from the Turkish by Talat Halman and Brian Swann

I

The story's told by a blind poet—
Before Troy even horses had souls.
Their neighings could be heard way down in Hades,
Horseless neighs making the dead shudder
And the dog frantic with fury.
At times hoofs drummed Trojan skies:
The restless soul of an unburied horse.

If the Achaeans had held the race for someone else that day
Achilles would have carried first prize to his hut,
For he owned immortal horses,
Poseidon's gift to his father Peleus
Who in turn passed them on to his son.
Now the horses mourn Patrocles,
Spirits broken, manes brushing earth.

Diomedes harnessed horses from Tros to his chariot,
Spoils from Aeneas
Whom a god had rescued.
Then fair-haired Menelaus, son of Atreus,

Godlike hero, rose and yoked two horses to his chariot:
Agamemnon's mare Aethe and his own horse Podargus.
Antilochus harnessed his horses from Pylos.
Then Rushen Ali the folk-hero mounted his Gray Horse
With wings on his flanks.
Distance had no meaning for him.
Then they brought out the haughty Wooden Horse.
Burning cedar spread all through the air;
Its magic scent disturbed the other horses.
Then Duldul appeared, Mohammed's gift to his son-in-law Ali;
Duldul the even-tempered mule, its genitals covered,
Walked slowly among the polytheistic horses.
Alexander's Bucephalus came next,
His head tilted, casting deep glances like Hindu girls.
From time to time he looked south,
As if he knew how near the Granicos flowed.
Then El Cid's Babieca appeared, and soon Rossinante showed up
Weeping.
                 Don't talk to me of horses!
I know they come from a mother's womb, at night, in the dark
Stable. Someone holds a lamp whose light flickers
On the straw. The mare coughs and pants,
Turns her head and looks: "Is he like me?
Are his fetlocks white?"
                 Don't talk to me of horses!
Like fields of morning severed from the earth,
Like its screaming cataracts, Pegasus leaps
The sky's chasm. My youth, my son!
It was a time of madness and mourning, vengeance of the dead,
Bodiless bird, shattered star, wound of forgotten rose,
Seedless little lakes rising like a monument of death,
And naked void, cowed space, that unending race . . . .
Horses, horses! I have never seen one grow old.
Some try toppling castles with their manes,
Some still scratch at the soil.
                 Don't talk to me of horses,
I can't bear the thought of them struck, struck down,
Defeated, lying on the ground, don't tell me,
Don't. I didn't see the Trojan War.

II   THE VENOM

Have you heard
What Mehmet the garage mechanic from Bursa has heard?
Because of his premonition that the city smelling
Of tar, fish, and pinewood, of an unsatisfied meadowlike woman,
Was to go up in flames,
Laocoön was bitten by the poisonous snake.
Women and children stood there writhing
On the shores of windy Ilion.
Remnants of death, scraps
Of life and love, heap on the shores,
The word lost and found in thought,
Infinity, like a searched-for broken statue.
Fame, greatness, and the enemy heap on the shores.
For the sea has not yet reached its fullness; it is sleepless
And half complete. It settles in its pierced barrel,
With its dregs of the ancient dead.

"On the bus coming back from the Izmir fair,
I saw Troy enveloped by a cloud."

They dumped all the books into gas chambers
In Dresden, Cologne, Munich.
Über allen gibfein ist Ruh . . .

"They say planes and birds are clashing in the sky,
Wings feathers beaks are raining on the city."

Have you heard?
All the girls in our brothels are foreign.
Their names are La, Li, Lu . . .

"All right.
What happened to the child left on the mountain?
Everyone's talking about this now.
Did animal or bird get him?
Couldn't we at least find his remains?

Couldn't we collect them and make up a person?
But then, what if he were left bodiless?
Could, couldn't, what if?"

III   THE DREAM

                              "Before dawn,
At the hour which, like an always hungry pigeon,
Picks up night's crumbs quickly,
When unborn children bend the bow of dreams,
The woman dreamed of child and fire."

"So they left the child on the mountain, where dream and fire
Lingered. If only they had left the dream behind."

"Yes, the dream frightened us, it had to be so,
We had no power not to interpret the dream
And do what we had to do.
The fire will wait until the child grows.
Let the crippled inscription of future days wait too,
And the mirror bloodied by bird beaks,

Wine is always aged and sipped,
Since blood gouts are red,
Day's color in ebb and flow, persisting song.
Haven't we split day into seven and night into five?
Haven't we sealed the waters of this sleepless resistance?
Haven't we flung the moon so far from birth,
Lengthened sleep's heavy funnel?
Let the reed wait in mysterious waters
And the eye-bird that peeps from the moon's skirt,
The blunt knife blinding the stone before the city's built,
Let them wait, the forehead destined to wait must wait.
I say hold on to the tide; it holds and waits.
Water, earth, the mind's wild weeds,
Merry-go-round, veils, temple and stairway endure,
Immortal happiness and boredom endure,
We wait, living what has been given us."

            "The Sage has suffered so much.

Do you suppose that together we can bear this anxiety
Which will last for unknown years?
We had no idea what our tomorrow would bring.
We still don't know, but this child is a hope,
The hope of our hopelessness.
>   Go and find him in the forest."

IV   THE TURNING

The forest's a magic net cast by naked natives,
And the mountain, like a hunted bewildered horse,
Struggles to cling onto life,
Climbs on and on toward the sky's hollow waters.
>   Down below,
Between walls and sea left desolate seven times,
Between the two wings of dream and fire,
Between day's front tooth and the shadow's rock,
Between the river's enduring dance, stretching time,
The single bullet of nothingness, which makes
Hasty willows speak death's tongue,
And the lake, the end's neighboring wall,
The horses kept turning . . . . I saw none that was aging.
Some try to topple towers with their manes,
Others still scratch the ground with their hoofs.
To one side the prize waited: a woman,
A tripod with handles, a six-year-old mare,
A cauldron untouched by fire, a two-handled kettle.
Shouts, sound of hoofbeats, clouds of dust . . . .
Über allen gibfein ist Ruh.

>   "All right, then,
What happened to the child left on the mountain?"

V   TELLING THE FUTURE

"See that blue bead? The other day
A camel driver held it. He was really strange.
He wanted his fortune told, but fearlessly
Fought against it. I don't understand. They say
He drowned crossing the Euphrates. Fortune's
A hungry dog—you chase it away, and back it comes
To find you. I pour lead to tell fortunes,
But whose fortune is this?
I told Macbeth he would be king: it didn't happen.
But I never told him he would kill the king.
It's not in my power to lengthen time either,
Nor shorten it. 'Yat sat tat ksanikam.'
Look, I blinked: all things were past and gone.
Tomorrow is yesterday, and yesterday has yet to come.
Let this bean be the child you hold: I push it.
It tumbles down the mountain. How long did it take?
I can't tell. I still can't tell if it's him or not.
Light a lamp. It gives one light in the evening,
A different one at midnight, still another before dawn,
But it's still the same lamp.
Santana ksana dharmas. Believe. Do not believe."

VI   LOVE

The forest would start when you held my hand,
split in two like a fig.
We would run up, bent double, breathless,
Tumbling with trout, pine-needles
Hindered our speed. Do not let go my hand. Do not let
Go my hand . . . .
            Then we'd slide all the way down,
And silence stooped like a tree,
Growing roots in us both, looking for
The soil's streams, one after the other.
Your sunflower breasts turned their faces to the light.
Like the hours of noon, I walked all over your breasts;
I walked on both sides of you like an arch of triumph.

Then we'd start running again,
Up, higher up, to the sky's hollow waters.
I'd kiss you and you'd tremble. Love
That unites broken moments sees no dream. Forest,
Fate of hunted horse, hungry pigeon of new beginnings!
We have no fortune to be told.
We burned it like a speck in the eyes of migrant birds
Or the single grain held in their beaks
At daybreak.
We have no fortune to be told.

GUSTAV HOLST COMPOSES HIMSELF

PAUL WEST

> Born in 1874, the composer Gustav Holst is
> best known for *The Planets*, which he never
> considered one of his best works; in fact, its
> popularity distressed him. A Virgo, and a
> vegetarian solitary who often subsisted on
> nuts, he had never heard the sound of a
> machine gun. His favorite emotional response
> was *Ohhh!*, and to autograph hunters he
> handed a slip of paper that said he did not
> give autographs. He studied Sanskrit, light-
> years, Trotsky and Jane Austen.—D. Ornulf,
> *A Compendium of Modern Music*

1

Every hour on the hour I go outside and comb it. Have you ever
done that with snow? It might have been sulphur or soot. Because
of what happened in 1923, in the second month, they called me
February Holst. I fell off a platform while conducting, struck the
back of my head, had slight concussion, but recovered, didn't die
until ten years later. I gather I became even austerer than usual
in those last years, I who neither drank nor smoked, who had
weak eyes and acute asthma, who rode a bicycle in the Algerian
desert as if I were in a double-doored soundproof room.

2

The housing here resembles a cheap stereo set. Black plastic top, with a dome through which I can just see the Pole Star. Any second, out of nowhere, maybe some quirk in the container, I expect a tone arm to flick out and plant its needle on my scalp to play me. As I revolve.

3

Never mind. The theory is banal. I had never realized that, after death, you live out all moments of blackout in miraculously transcendent fits arranged for you at notable sites on the planet.

4

I wince at that last word still, liked only *Saturn*, bringer of old age.

5

There's a logic, though. They told me as I squirmed, the co-opted and half-dead engrams: *Rage not, February Holst. Ordinary sleep excepted, blackout entitles you to extra time. As investment or reprieve. A stay at least. You are not alone. To wit: before he finally died, Franz Kafka spent a month in a zoo in Tashkent; Homer many nods' lengths in a bottle of dark burgundy. Charles Ives did time inside the elbow of a wrist-wrestler from Biloxi.* Imagine the humiliation, the pain. One has to soldier through life's leftovers.

6

I go outside and comb it again with tortoise-shell foot-long manual plow, suitable for outsize St. Bernard. Little scintillants clot my leather-clad hand. It might be hell. It varies. I was out, after my fall, about half an hour, and thereafter I suppose I had intermittent blanks totaling only a week. It will soon be over, then. I think of Beethoven's tuning fork, which I once owned, but gone it is.

7

Nine things I've already had to do.
Go out and capture a bloated pancreas as it caromed over the snow. Then drag it in, thaw it with body heat. (It burst.)
Catch, by reaching up, a pearl-feathered polar bird, its head phthisic and sharp. (Hugged it, ate it.)
Hum my very own *Ode to Death*, a dirge of frosted air. (Awful.)

Keep pressing thumb print into disc of gold leaf provided. (As evidence?)

Collect up dung of polar bears. (For fuel? But where's the flame?) Also danced a sarabande. Quoted ghosts. Bit lip, thus moving my blood like a sleepwalker tasting sweat.

8

A long sleigh laden with pensive giraffes halts above the dome. A rope ladder falls, down which treads the giraffe-master, a Pickwick with Dali mustachios, clad in samite parka. He finger-writes on the dome in such a way that I can read it. *I know, I know,* I sing up at him, *I have been weighed in the balance and found—* the fat-head nods, then drapes over the dome a terminal moraine of eye-teeth, eggshells, and arsenical green grit. My last view is of the giraffes thwacking their necks together. In farewell? Or were they wooing one another? Genius is the recovery of childhood by will.

9

I have just come in from cleaning the dome, rope round my waist so as not to blow away. Like one space-walking. On Betelgeuse the gold leaves hang in golden aisles for twice a hundred billion miles. Time is a bird that does not fly, space a wind that cannot blow.

10

A bar's rest at last. In the old days, I even had a special nib fitted to my finger, lest the neuritis . . . .

11

Yet it's not that badly appointed a place. There's an ice-phone connected by some filament or ribbon of aerial snail-track to the roof. I have a crevasse toilet, an oubliette all icicles. Bed is fox-fur on five staves. A crystal skillet matches a glass punch ladle. Books made of lovely impacted Arctic blue flowers (I surmise) fill a skin shelf. I walk on a crossword embedded in the floor, black to white ice and back, but cluelessly get nowhere. Jitter-shivers quake me.

Mercy, did the whole edifice just now move round? Rotate through fifteen degrees or so? Towards the right.

There it goes again, through half a right angle.

They'll spin me to a second death, then, centrifuge to blackout. Or will it be red?

12

It's stopped. Is this mysticism? The drop and the ocean? I'm like the light in the mausoleum.

13

No time to wonder. Here they come, not giraffes but, wafting in like phantoms over the transom of the possible, toys. A Parthenon, in tungsten, stands to attention, grimmer than when it once sang to me in the Greek light. Mozart, squatting on a breakfast tray, scribbles an overture while his wife upon his shoulder tells him tales to keep him awake. And Ralph Vaughan Williams, once friend, shambles at me like a dinosaur, cries *Sled!* Then a crowd of people all facing Rubens, I know not why. On top of all that comes a red London bus labeled TYROL.
Ho, I whisper, winningly.
Who goes there? snaps the Parthenon.
I say my name.
A wobbling bus runs over it.
Reprieved, I faintly mouth; but the crowd facing Rubens turn away as one, board their bus, shove me away as from a mass grave.

14

Ah, could I now address myself c/o Poste Restante, Dresden. I am frail. But too much is clear.

15

This. I went to Jesus but I didn't drink. He was truly nice and kept me an hour and a half. My soul has naught but fire and cold. (Then where's the fire?) My soul has come unshod. Even the *Bhagavad-Gita* let me down. It's never enough to be religious. You have to want to be wrong.

16

And your blunders come back in diary form: "Mildness is the very devil." I said it. And "Art is not the sum total of its details." I drank to that. Then: "Form without inspiration is only cold storage." Is that what did it? Or my crack about "boiling inspiration" and how bad it was for music.

17

I didn't fathom life; and, if this is death, I'm puzzled still. Is Delius an orange? Has Hindemith been incorporated into the Isenheim altar? Is Bruckner a Viennese coin? Why am I thus singled out? Circumstanced as I, what would *you* do with *your* stay of execution? I sing my geode, my Earth-Ode, as best I can, tossing fragments of snowball at you. Duck.

18

Teeth chattering, I hear the moral of the heartbeat: *Compose yourself*, an asinine order, followed by dread words in combination. Can it be I'm hearing the sounds of Mars?
Feuersnot.
box.
the White Viennese Band.
oils.
Berlin 1903.
Lovely Venus.
bleeding ulcers.
Thaxted Church, Essex.
morphine.
heart fibs.
10 The Terrace, Barnes.
Old Thames, Old Man River.
I was due to go to Honolulu.
I might yet.

19

Propped up on two pillows, with two eggs a day, in my bloody middle sixties, I wrote to a friend: When you visit the British Museum, mind you see the picture of the family going across to Paradise and having afternoon tea on the raft while other relatives wave a welcome from the shore. Such images uplift.

20

At this late date, I wish a pox on all planets, yours and mine, theirs, his and hers, especially His. I'm adjusting poorly. I'm not adjusting at all. I'm poorly.

21

Oh, ye hags of night. Am I a paradox-monger or an ass? When a youth, I answered a bird's whistle and was answered back. It wanted me to mate. I slid its beak up my nostril, I sat its plumage on my lap. I have always been timid.

22

A moment of authentic terror just then. The thing I comb reared up outside, with beautifully developed spiral neck and throat; but untold brutalities rest on the upper lip, which flows into a snout, a mouthless gargoyle, for nostril there is none. And through the temple in the skull a shaft or ravine drives deep into the brain where rich, umbrageous cowflaps float Sargasso-like. *Hass!* I cry, stealing from Berlioz, *The Damnation of Faust.* Then *Irimiru! Karabrao!* Purloined shrieks; no ordinary words will do. I fall upward into a cone of gulls.

23 Overture

I go outside and again comb it. I think it knows me. With its bleached, saber-shag flank, it heaves a welcome as I part the cold snags and split the matted stuff. I stay out, ready to move off when its trust has bloomed, it with snowcapes round its furred meniscus, I with my igloo head and five-toothed currycomb.

SIX POEMS

GAVIN EWART

WHERE THE ACTION IS

On the lawn of the beautiful country house
where Lady Menopause
is serving a dogshit sandwich.

DARK CONSOLATION

Even the little battered baby,
as it lies dying in its cot,
has known moments of happiness.

THE SEXUAL SIGH

The small buttocks of men, that excite the women . . .
but ah! the beautiful feminine broadness!

SONNET: LIBERATED

After a certain time all wives, when
their husbands are dead (or separated) and the children have
                                                    left home,
give a big sigh of relief—for now they can start to *live*:
go to pottery classes, have young men as lovers,
live with their sisters, do gardening or go to the opera.
They feel free, they don't have ever again
to work like slaves for a selfish family.
This is the Shangri-La, the Promised Land.

Snoring, boring, farting, tarting, drinking, stinking
are all good adjectives for husbands, in the Book of Wives.
The daughters are sluts and the sons are layabouts
but they don't have to worry about them any more,
they've done their duty. They're free! It's wonderful! Free!
Sometimes they wonder why they ever got married.

A GENTLEMAN CONGRATULATES A LADY
ON HER BREASTS (1890)

I knew they would be nice, even before I met them
(socially, as it were),
and now I would find it impossible to forget them
(such a perfect pair),
after being introduced, to handle them and kiss them.
I know that I should miss them

if they travelled abroad, or became inaccessible
for some other reason—
the delight they bring me is quite unassessable—
if for the Season
they took a house in a London square, and dances
laid them open to advances

by philanderers with impertinent whiskers,
the experienced men,
or athletes finely built to throw the discus,
oh then, dear, then
at the thought of the pear-drop large areolas
I should grind my molars

in jealousy that they should be exposed there
to lascivious eyes
or that exploring fingers should be closed there,
occasioning sighs,
making the Classical scholars exclaim in Latin!
Oh, safe beneath the satin

please keep them there, quite hidden from the vulgar
and lesser breeds,
foreign Ambassadors, Greek, Turk or Bulgar,
all alien creeds,
each paunchy pompous prying Silenus!
Sacred to me and Venus,

like Gilbert and Sullivan or Castor and Pollux,
the heavenly twins,
identical like (soldiers' words) Mars's bollocks,
the couple that wins
divine approval, till I wake them with kisses
keep them like Moslem misses!

YOU ARE THE ONE

You are the one
for whom the swallows fly
in V-formations,
for whom the chestnut candles
        burn there so gently,
You are the one

You are the one
for whom the breezes bend
when ice is forgotten,
for whom the daffodils
          raven like lions,
You are the one

You are the one
for whom the newness comes,
to please you with mating,
for whom the lambs are light
          beating the pasture,
You are the one

You are the one
for whom the earth renews,
overcoats are discarded,
for whom like a flame-coloured dress
          there are gladioli,
You are the one

You are the one
for whom the bright sun shines,
to move you into a smile,
for whom the moon gravely
          makes amusing patterns,
You are the one

You are the one
for whom the organs rejoice
and breasts are identical twins,
for whom there is singing
          and intricate dances,
You are the one

You are the one
for whom the bees offer praise,
and your thighs are delicious,
for whom the dead Romans
          made hymns in Latin,
You are the one

You are the one
for whom the trains run South
as your gaze is delightful,
for whom the iced martinis
              are poured in plenty,
You are the one

You are the one
for whom the blood presses upwards,
keen to intrigue you,
for whom there are festivals
              and off-duty laughter,
You are the one

You are the one
for whom the whole world is a plaything;
to tickle your fancy
for you the ostrich feathers
              soothe your soft smoothness,
You are the one

You are the one
for whom the stretched earth is a hammock
where you lie lovely,
for whom we are stupid with homage,
              in face of your beauties,
You are the one

You are the one.

THRU

An excerpt from the novel Thru

CHRISTINE BROOKE-ROSE

AUTHOR'S NOTE: Thru *is not really a novel, nor a novel about a novelist writing a novel, but a text about the textuality of a text or, at most, a fiction about the fictionality of fiction, a "see-through" text.*

It opens with words patterned in puns, acrostics, allusions (for all texts arise out of others) working through and through each other as they might form in an author's mind or, as Yeats put it, "out of a mouthful of air," and slowly get constituted into a narrative, though this is only apparent. Two main characters seem to be inventing each other, but as any one episode gets going the text itself destroys it. Sometimes the narrator appears to be Larissa, sometimes Armel, sometimes someone else or even an omniscient narrator. Other times the narrator turns out to be different students in a creative writing class and once (here) he is the Master in Diderot's Jacques le Fataliste.

Thru is about language as a driving mirror, into which you look ahead to see backwards, until you're overtaken.—C. B-R.

So far however there are no actant-places except the Other Scene and the Institution of Learning where the old learn from the young and the young learn nothing until suddenly one day they too are old. And even that has just been closed down by an arbitrary act of Authority after serious textual disturbances due to the obscurity of excessive generalisation.

Some universities have large square rooms for faculty meetings with bottom-shaped chairs and liftable side-flaps for left-minded people not to write on a point of information, some have board-room tables. In some you lecture on a raised dais in an amphib-iantheatre to a sea of floating faces rising in waves upward and away, in some you sit ensconced in an armchair protected all around by walls of books, in others you sit on a table among the students but so as to be above them nevertheless and casually chat. In some you peripat along in ancient sunshine (known also as the peripatetic fallacy), in others you walk up to one who sits by the roadside pretending to be receiving wisdom and say you old fool, come out of it, get up and do something useful, you sit on the one and only wooden Chair between St Julien le Pauvre and Notre Dame or is it Ali Nourennin and Saroja Chaitwantee with the students on sacks of straw under a leaden sky. Now and then the mosaic of bent heads breaks and the boulevards which were orig-inally promenades constructed out of demolished bulwarks are bouleversed back into bulwarks again. Other times the bulldozers are content to crash into the timetable. In some actant-places you have chalk and sponge and blackboard to inscribe and scrub your diagrams, in others a roll of parchment from which you dictate figures of rhetoric or else an organ of flash buttons facing glass cubicles full of earphoned heads or an overhead projector and a spirit-loaded pen which you dip into your mind coming at this moment upon nothing at all in the sudden isolation of losing I-contact with everyone except set pieces of masterpieces dying or half dead. There are degrees of presence just as there are de-grees of redundancy to save the message from entropy which is the negative measure of the significance of the message. These are familiar rules, made to be broken in an age of transition between evolving permanence and permanent revolution moving right to left from the point of view of the object exchanged.

Order order. You don't have the floor it's Larissa's turn.

I am astounded. I think it is quite aberrant, not to mention confusing, for first year students to be plunged into Generative Grammar in one class and Black Protest or Women's Lib in an-other. For one thing the Women's Lib lot don't understand a thing about deep structures and are crashing around with destructive naivety but that's a parenthesis Larissa that's not fair. I can't have you will you let me finish please. You are turning this place into a carnival. Well I have no objection it's a mode of perception as Bakhtine has shown, but you should then be aware that carnival has its own structure at every level all taboos suspended all hierarchy reversed and certain very specific ineluctible processes I forebear to mention. There is too, the question of duration. If you know what you're doing, fine, go ahead. But I doubt it. And if we must have this chaotic freedom in the choice of courses let us at least integrate it through psychic structures that we understand. A text is a text is a text.

What on earth are you talking about?

Yes if you're going to hold that kind of discourse please explain yourself.

This is not the place.

The bar functions like a shrug of scorn between signifier and signified for ever eluded and played out elsewhere, in some other class perhaps where revolution that has been long preparing out of archaic flaws in the dialectic of change raises antinomies of action that surpasses the subjective and renders it objective so that men realise retrospectively that they have accomplished more than they desired and worked at something infinitely beyond them, making a turntable of the timetable so that, twiddling along the transistor you dip in but not too deep (but why at this precise point?) where neither workers nor women let alone coloured people have gained anything by so-called emancipation and the double standard remains. Left wing intellectuals talk a lot about making the revolution like it was making love and about destroying capitalism and the consumer society but they don't for all that refrain from enjoying consumer goods or borrowing vast sums at a high interest to buy luxury flats uptown and a country house in the bargain. As Marcuse said even the proletariat has been bribed so that we now have a new proletariat of second-rate citizens since any capitalist society must have a slave population, nor does one notice the intellectuals objecting to that. Or take women—leaving aside the bourgeoisie and their well-known mythologies one finds the very same intellectuals who talk of revolution and endorse black and women's lib having as mistresses young teachers or graduate students who slave willingly, for example at compiling an index for their man's thesis or next publication or typing it. But who ever heard of a man doing the index for a female graduate's thesis or typing it? As for sexual liberty well, the double standard is rampant everywhere one is amazed. If the woman objects she is being hysterical and making a scene. But the man objects in much more fundamental and subtly unpleasant ways, disguising it as high-mindedness of some sort. I know of one case not so far away in which a man who lives with a young teacher has installed another, from the same department of course, expecting them to live in love and peace with great talk of communal life and the new ideology. Fine but when she says OK the same for me he won't hear of it. Where's the new ideology in that? It's as old as sultans and no doubt cavemen. He even has them both working on his Index (laughter) and typing it. The more fool them.

Women in fact have gained all the responsibilities of men and none of their privileges, losing their own while men have lost something too, their sense of responsibility. And that at least was not the trouble in the days of the tyrant father. And even typical psychic castrates like Don Juan and Casanova at least were not hypocrites. In the Don Juan myth—the symbolic structure of which has long ago been analysed as that of castration, that of a man marked with the sign of incompleteness—the hero is at least magnificent to the end and it's the others who are left bathetically moralising by the fire of hell, nor does he treat his women as nannies to solve his problems or as harem-slave-secretaries, though of course his repetitive pattern of continual conquest by means of wild promises is an attempt to solve them at another level, and doomed to failure. But if he's a small winner he's at least a great loser. That's, that's all. I—I meant to develop it a bit more but I didn't have time.

Mmmm. That's, very interesting. There are some good ideas there Doreen. The—er—levels of discourse are a bit mixed up though, aren't they? What do you think, er, Eliza?

What I mean is, there are several voices in Doreen's essay, and maybe some of them jar a bit. Now which, do you think, and why?

Come along now, this is a free discussion. We'll leave the facts aside for the moment, but what is it that gives a sort of wrong tone here, not, shall we say, very scholarly or objective?

Well she don' pay no tension to the black people cep for the everlastin white lip-servus.

Right. But then she wasn't supposed to deal with that was she?

She mentioned it at the beginning as a parallel, like the workers, but this is on Women's Lib. That's not what I meant.

At all, that is not it at all. Who speaks? Isabel perhaps or Claire who teaches the Inscription of Protest. For the significance of any message is synonymous with its information within a system of probability as opposed to entropy and disorder. But information depends on its emitter so that a message however predictable such as condolence would increase its level of information to an extraordinary degree if it came from the president of the counsel of ministers of the USSR or the Emperor of China, information being related to improbability, which is why modern novels can be so disorientating despite the fact that through this chaotic freedom in the network of possibilities we fill the air with noises, twiddle along the timetable from left to right and back, from one disembodied voice to another on this or that wave-length listening in to this or that disc-jockey and always the same disc-horse, a yea-yea and a neigh inserted into the circuit of signifiers, each discourse penetrating the non-disjunctive functioning of another. And we do not find that concert disconcerting. The greater the noise the greater the redundancy has to be. Go forth and multiply the voices until you reach the undecidable even in some psychoasthmatic amateur castrate who cannot therefore sing the part.

Ah. A self-evident defence-mechanism against threat of extermination. Why this flight into delirious discourse?

But now it is quite clear who speaks: the man from Porlock. He has been speaking for some time.

He comes, in fact, from Timbuctoo in Mali, half way between the Niger and Lake Faguibin longitude 03 West latitude 17 North. He is slight and mighty, mat brown and dazzling—a chance occurrence yet clearly also generated by anticipation at the flick of a timetable, so that makes everything all right despite the interruption—and the lines of his hands like the skin between the fingers are deadly greyish white because, he says when rudely asked by way of tacitactic diversion, he has been cleaning something with a strong detergent. He is cultrate and cultivated, ebullient and bullying, censorious and sensitive, tactless and tactile (tu me le paieras ce maudit portrait) from which several facts you will have gathered that he is a writer.

Do white writers then get black lines on their hands when they clean things up?

Of course, look.

That's ink, too much.

Et pourquoi haïssez-vous les portraits?

C'est qu'ils ressemblent si peu, que, si par hasard on vient à recontrer les originaux

Don't tell me you belong to the critical school that ferrets around seeking Dorothea's husband and the model for the Wife of Bath?

Who's Bath? Do you mean Barthes?

The bell rings. The pen is put down in mid-sentence

which one?

Guess. The eye is put to the judas-eye

you mean the trait-or master of the moment I mean the markster of the comment who dreams things up?

and there he is, curiously foreshortened by the lens, carrying five books, including one of yours foolishly loaned on a pressing request

do you mean one of yours or one of mine?

I didn't know you'd written any I mean one of yours I speak in the second person

which means one of yours why don't you say so

I do if you will allow me to proceed

proceed

The moment of hesitation passes, the door opens

on its own?

in some languages things do themselves

aha! l'amor si fa?

that is not what I meant at all may I for Chrissake bring this person in who is as I have said, a man.

Well if you put it that way get on with it, there can be no breaking in before the breaking of the lock no wonder you call him the man from Porlock.

There are times, Jacques, when the recipient should be shot right out of the message he makes so much noise.

Ah but where would the message be without him that's why redundancy was invented come to think of it it's easier for the emitter to disappear if things do themselves.

So far there is neither emitter nor recipient within the message, only without, thanks to you.

All right silence pax proceed hands across the sea

Hello.

I want to talk to you.

Fine beginning I must say
I wither him with a look.

I'm writing.

I know.

I'm seeing no-one, I don't answer the door.

The door hasn't said anything, and you have answered.

Well because I knew you knew I was here and I didn't want to offend you.

She who explains herself is lost. May I come in?

She?

Yes, you gave me an idea.

Ah.

Well, yes of course, what er can I do for you? Would you like a drink? Have a cigarette. Or some coffee or

No no sit down. Give me your hand.

Why?

I want to talk to you

Can't you talk without touching? What about?

Well of course about your book which I have touched handled read look I have taken all these notes.

But I only gave it to you a couple of hours ago you can't have read it.

Ah the vanity of authors. I am an author.

So I hear, and very successful.

Oh that, I don't care. Give me your hand.

Look, I only met you this morning

You mean there is a timetable in white society for hand-holding?

Well yes. I didn't even properly catch your name.

Armel.

What?

Armel.

Oh.

And yours?

It's on the book and on my door.

Ah but it might be a pseudonym. Larissa. That's nice. Larissa Toren. It almost sounds African.

Please, I'm in the middle of a sentence

which one?

I've already forgotten it thanks to you. Tell me what you want to say.

A great deal. It will take a long time. Come and have a kouskous with me.

I'm sorry I've already eaten and I'm working.

Not now you are not.

Please say it now then.

Why this flight?

What flight?

That's what I asked myself all the time while reading your book look I have made notes. The publisher says it's very funny. He's mad.

That's not part of the book don't you know what a blurb is? The publisher says that to sell it and you're quite right, he fails. It has nothing to do with the text.

Ah. In my countries publishers tell the truth.

I didn't know you had publishers there aren't you published in America?

We don't, that's why they don't have to lie.

Hmm. So you don't think it funny?

Ah that hurt did I? Of course it's not funny you are weeping all the time it is one long cry of anguish.

Oh?

This woman for instance she says page 143, no, it's somewhere else, well never mind what I mean is there are moments when you touch on the very essence of things and then brrt! you escape, you run away into language. You are merely amusing yourself and I want to know why.

You mean that when I touch on the essence of things, in that text, it's not by means of language? What is it then?

There you go again, playing with words. Why this flight?

Into logic? Look, this is ridiculous, charming but ridiculous. Aren't you playing with words too, doesn't everyone?

Not me. Give me your hand.

No. So. I'm weeping all the time and yet I'm merely amusing myself. But isn't the only thing to do with a long cry of anguish to amuse oneself? In my country we never separate the two. I take it as a compliment. But you seem to utter these phrases as reproaches.

No, no, please do not take offence. Ah writers are so sensitive, I know, I am sensitive and now you are treating me as a person of no sensibility.

Oh come, we're both above exchanging hurt sensibilities.

That's better. Come, give me your hand.

No. Why do your hands have white lines?

Don't yours? Show me.

No.

Yes they have. See?

They're not white, they're beige, same as the hands, a bit darker if anything. Whereas yours

I have been cleaning something with a strong detergent. This is my natural colour, here, look.

What do you do when you write?

I use language, yes, I admit. But directly.

That's an old illusion. But I didn't mean that, I meant, do you cut yourself off?

Cut myself! Oh you mean, oh yes, completely, I rip out the telephone and see no one.

Well then can't you understand

But I want to understand that's why I came. Here you give me this book

because you happened to be at my neighbour's whom I happened to see on the stairs and who happened to ask me in and happened to introduce me to you and happened to insist that you should read one of my books

that's a lot of happening it must mean something

on the contrary it's a string of chance improbabilities. A terminal string.

and I happened to come up and want to discuss it with you so that you will perhaps happen not to take this flight any more

which is likely to have the opposite effect. Listen, you're very nice but I wrote this book ages ago it's dead and gone for me. I know everything that's wrong with any book I write by the time it comes out. I am now in the middle of another and to hear anything at all, for or against, about an earlier one is simply imp— nonpertinent, irrelevant I mean. But the interruption isn't, it could block me for days.

Ah, you see, you do care.

As you care about success.

That's a completely different level.

It isn't what you say it's the fact of interruption. A friend from Morocco turned up the other day

my country is near Morocco. There is only the whole of Algeria in between.

and I couldn't not see him. It was delightful. It took two hours. I lost three days.

Because that was real. It takes a lot of trouble and concentration to construct your escapist edifice.

Look, er, Armel, you're very perceptive, but you're not the only one to say these things you know, I've heard them before, many times.

You see. I'm in the majority then.

The majority doesn't make the truth.

A reactionary into the bargain.

Don't be silly. You think you know me from quickly leafing through a book.

I have read it all from cover to cover. And taken notes.

The majority also prefers platitudes. And I'm sick and tired of this one about language as an escape from reality. Language is all we have to apprehend reality, if we must use that term. And I notice that when people talk of reality they usually mean sex, with them.

Now Larissa Toren author, that is naughty, you are jumping to conclusions, I was referring uniquely to the communication you had with your Moroccan friend. But here you are putting delicious ideas into my innocent head.

And if they don't mean sex they mean communication. As if communication wasn't language.

Yes yes my dear but what language? I brought these other books to show you: here is a best-seller and sometimes you write like it. Sometimes however you write like this one, here, which is, look, I took all these notes.

All discourse is the return of a discourse by the Other, without whom I am not, but to whom I am more attached than to myself, I say I but I mean everyone, all of us, nor can I proceed to the identification of that I except through the medium of language.

There you go again.

Why do you suppose patients talk, and write? Why did the silent movies have captions? Why does teaching continue through books and dialogues and not simply by means of gestures and diagrams and experiments in glass bottles?

Well they do seem to use more and more diagrams but that's precisely

Why for that matter did you come up to talk if it wasn't to use language about language?

To go beyond your book.

to undermine it with other language, and that's fine, you have every right, everyone has a right to subvert any text with any other but now

and to hold your hand

well and so you have. And now truly I must put you out and get on with my work.

You are escaping again. All right you are the host I must submit. You know there is an ancient Peruvian substitute for writing by knotting threads. It is called Quipu.

Sauve qui peut then.

Ah Larissa Toren author come give me a kiss.

No.

Larissakissammmmmmmmmmmmmmm.

That's enough. Now please be a good boy and go.

And when can I see you again? Will you come and have a kous-kous with me?

Bang—bang?

Excuse me?

I'm sorry but I don't like kous-kous.

You don't like kous-kous!

Well it's too greasy for me I don't digest it.

I'll have something else for you then. What do you like? When will you come?

Next winter.

You are mad. I shall not be here next winter.

Too bad.

I mean now please Larissa Toren author surely you have to eat sometimes?

I'm sorry. In any case I'm expecting my husband any day, to-night perhaps.

You have a husband! Ah well, now I understand everything.

Good. You might have found that out from my neighbour. Goodbye. Thanks for calling.

Which could be called society as a subversion of the text, if it were not itself textual.

You see even the hands were unnecessary in the portrait.

Jacques my friend you must help me. Certain problems have arisen.

Yes master?

Well, first,

Oh no master, not that firstly fourthly on the one hand small a small b stuff I can't take it in. All right at faculty meetings but not when I have to participate.

Okay scrub it then one equals zero.

Please master what is the problem?

I'm just telling you. To begin with, I mean, sorry scrub that. Thanks to the man from Timbuctoo it is clear that Larissa is producing a text. But which text? It looks mightily as if she were producing this one and not, as previously appeared, Armel, or Armel disguised as narrator or the narrator I disguised as Armel. That's not very clear.

No it isn't.

Of course she may be producing a different text.

She may indeed, master.

That's not very clear either.

Perhaps not.

But you see what follows from that?

Not quite yet master.

It means that the narrator I transformed into Larissa am no longer your master but your mistress.

Master! I find that most offensive. I know that we quarrelled at the inn, but I made you agree afterwards that all our quarrels were due to our not accepting the fact that although you were pleased to call yourself and I was pleased to call you the master, I am in fact yours. And when you asked me where I had learnt such things I replied in the great book, which seemed to settle the matter. But no great book could justify, in our long relationship (which I may remind you includes the story of my loves, much interrupted but otherwise normal and healthy) no great book as I say could justify the imputation you have just made. I beg leave therefore, although it breaks my heart, to part company once and for all with one who

Jacques, Jacques, stop that. I didn't mean it literally.

Literally is I hope precisely how you did mean it master.

Jacques! You are a genius. Of course it was literal. A question of textuality.

There you go again.

Heterotextuality of course.

Eh?

It was a manner of speaking.

And a very strange manner if I may say so.

Well let's forget it there are more important problems than my change of, I mean thirdly, no I mean, to get back to the subject of discourse, this woman Larissa has not only usurped my place as narrator, which apart from putting our relationship in danger

you said to forget it

I placed it in a parenthesis—poses other problems. On the one hand, I mean for one thing her mental diagrams may be a good deal more complex than mine, but that's my problem, and on the other she has also acquired a sudden husband as a last minute escape.

He could be a polite lie.

Yes but he could be vero, no?

A husband is always, from a woman's point of view, ben trovato.

You are speaking like an eighteenth century man-servant.

Yes I am. And you are an eighteenth century gentilhomme.

But in the late twentieth century, Jacques, women have been liberated, as you heard, and it is therefore only a man's archaic viewpoint that his name and person are the greatest boons he can confer upon a woman.

Ah.

Oh don't start that A E I O U business again be articulate this is serious.

Yes master.

Of course her husband if true would have to be Armel

But she's only just met him and told him

no that's a coincidence. They do happen despite the critics.

I don't think so. You know my answer to all our problems, which has given me my surname

not your surname your epithet

if it is written above

that's striking below the belt

if as I say it is written up there that we are to quarrel again, and make it up again, and have sexual problems

textual

textual problems that tie us up in knots like er Quipu, then it is also written that knots are meant to be either disentangled or cut.

Jacques what would I do without you?

That's what I said at the inn. And before you opened the door into the narrative.

Not only are they meant to be disentangled they are themselves meaningful. Decipherable.

Oh decisively.

Of course her surname is different. For you may not have noticed that she has acquired a surname from the book he was holding. That's no problem in the twentieth century though. But it's oddly close isn't it? Toren, Santores, why, it's part of it! And that's why they write letters they're separated-but-very-good-friends.

Well didn't you know that? It's the only thing which is clear, the epistolary novel is always crystal clear people will explain themselves. But what about Armel?

Yes, that doesn't quite fit. Moreover her mental diagrams seem to be also a good deal more complex than his, though his emotional ones seem more complex than hers, which is perhaps the trouble, but poses another problem if she is inventing him, and even more so if he is inventing her. Still, we'll come to that. As to the first name, well of course she could have changed whatever original name she gave to the man she was inventing, maybe it was Marco or Stavro, hence the confusion of brows hair and height at the beginning, and given him the name of the man from Porlock, I mean from Timbuctoo.

I don't follow.

To get something out of the interruption if only an unusual name.

You said women don't want a name from a man in the twentieth century.

Oh for fictional purposes yes.

Ah. I mean, so nothing has changed then, in the twentieth century?

That's the whole point, you see, out of the zero where the author is situated, both excluded and included, the third person is generated, pure signifier of the subject's experience. Later this third person acquires a proper name, figure of this paradox, one out of zero, name out of anonymity, visualisation of the fantasy into a signifier that can be looked at, seen. You should read Kristeva that's what she says. Though we mustn't forget that in the grammar of narrative the proper name coincides with the agent. In this way the construction of a character has to pass through a death, necessary to the structuring of the subject as subject of utterance, and for his insertion into the circuit of signifiers, I mean the narration. It is therefore the recipient, you Jacques, or anyone, the other, who transforms the subject into author, making him pass through this zero-stage, this negation, this exclusion which is the author. I am in fact dead, Jacques. Oh, he's asleep. What a pity. Everything is becoming clear at last. God! No! Yes! Quick, pen and paper

ARMEL   SANTORES
LARISSA   TOREN

Yes! It figures. So that's why she said about Armel not finding his ME in her and she not finding her I. Why the names are anagrams. Except for ME in hers and I in his. Am I going mad? Help! I should have stuck to pronouns as in late twentieth century texts which refuse biographies since a name must have a civic status. In the pluperfect. Or a camouflashback pluperfect. That's the rule. Written up there. In the grammar of narrative. Like attributes—states, properties and statuses. Iterative is opposed to actions. But any agent can enter into relationship with any predicate. The notions of subject and object correspond only to a place in the narrative proposition and not to a difference in nature hence no need to talk like Propp et al of hero villain lawbearer these are predicates. The agent is not the one who can accomplish this or that action but the one who can become subject of a predicate. Hence only proper names, not substantives, though of course there can be duplication as when three brothers or robbers accomplish an identical action they are syntactically speaking one agent just as two lovers can be temporarily united in one proposition. So there have to be proper names after all, Jacques, Jacques why are you asleep?

No, no master, I was listening.

Jacques. I am going to break all the commandments.

Oh good. When?

Well—tomorrow. First I must sleep. Undress me Jacques. I'm very very tired. Dead in fact.

Yes master. Come, your redingote. There. Now let me unbutton the waistcoat. One, two, three, four

oh make haste Jacques.

Well there are a lot of buttons. There.

That's enough I'll sleep like this I'm falling already

But master, your jabot, your boots Oh Lord he's off. See you later I-narrator. Here we go, left foot, yeeeeeeeeank. Right foot, yeeeeeeeeeank.

Mmmmm. Sing me a lullaby Jacques.
Anon anon sir. Ahem.

> Rock a narrator
> On a phrase-top
> When the verb blows
> The tree-structure will rock
> When the noun breaks
> The tree-structure will fall
> Down comes the noun-phrase narrator and all

into an idyll
and about time too

VARIATIONS DONE FOR GARY SNYDER

CLAYTON ESHLEMAN

At the point the earth contracts a beautiful emphasis?
Consciousness a two-way street by a one-way polluted stream
Kyoto dirty chessboard
    I passed in snow the first night farawayland fairyland
This is something else I felt deep in the warmth of the cab
                looking out
Iced stream flowing into a birth, I started to say a bridge
    I started to say driving along that little dream north of
              Kyoto Station
Barbara was there We didn't know where we were going
The grasp for one phrase to make you see
    what I never will see again, new country
tangled in the legs I am trying to cross uncross in my lap

At the point consciousness reverses a tree turns within its
              own bark?
Have I spat out Clayton while the polluted sky mainlined the
              beech?
Have you Gary integrated Kitkitdizze while our sister the eel
    can no longer regurgitate Mercury?
At the point the earth contracts do we suddenly see how we
              can live?

The spiderweb dangles vulva-outward its fibers
  An 80 year old man sleeps on the sidewalk
becomes conscious as a sun-tentacle gropes around his eyes
The octopus sun, the erotic sun
   that in young men smashes a chink out of their unlit cells
For the old man the ray was "the most beautiful sunrise I

              have ever

  seen in my life" Not an aggression
but a filmy dragon of reception
The storks at play in the lotus pond
The immense need of the Chinese to feel the peach
  swollen with jade

I try to hold in mind one thought: the earth in contraction
An LA backyard of pastel screens in which the fir and lemon tree
  parts of a set
can be moved into a film or be replaced by a person
Rebirth so passionately meaningful
  In the orgone accumulator
overgrown with ivy, the goat-god inside coupled with darkness
  Brothel walls of Pompei so smooth now one
  can hardly hear this hoarse chortle

        those heavy heavy Paris
curtains, the lead velvet folds increasingly an oviduct where

         a tentacle
drowses, leaves a part of itself, the arm of
a hundred suckers, Mauthausen with its Blond Damsel

Not a contraction like a blow in the stomach or even a birth wince
The ache a feeling of the grass growing in each blade more narrow
So that the line narrows, there is less concentration on
any one focus, movement is freer, the horror is skipped over
We don't have to contract as Baudelaire did plum blossom poison
or be possessed by maggots with Greek statues in their arms
   The bag of vipers loosed on an island
that thrash around and are called critics, who self-populate
and then swim off to the shores where we are
caught with our gods down, I mean our poems halfway out the only
way a poem can truly stay for a moment glistening in the sun

Ixcuina the Aztec inspiration crouched
a world then utterly open it seems now
but they would cut a woman's lips off her face
about as fast as I threw the squeezed half of a lemon at Caryl
Our world in contraction and that Aztec woman under
a skullrack in bloodclothes 6 days without moisture or light
                          Each movement must be
                          justified, aligned, by its contrary
                          to be created in the text
                          The Red Lotus peak
                          must be imbued with juice
                          from under her tongue
                          The Double Lotus Peak
                          must carry the meaning of
                          milk spit from tits unchildsucked
                          The Peak of the Purple Fungus
          ah! can only hide the
                    Grotto of the White Tiger, gateway to
the depths of Sanjusangendo where archers
work daylightlong behind 1001 peaks of molten casts
Just to hear the arrows fly all day long, the endurance,
                                        the winner the most
arrows shot through
not a single most accurate
chessmove, clear green Kyoto!
An Indiana boy is beckoning his girlfriend out of that rancid
Sanjusangendo, breaking her from her caste, since she is lively
and wonderful and touched with devotion he can feel the
                                        misguided
sculptor who 1000 years ago sealed her in a mental iron
                                        maiden called
Kannon, weaving the key into the tightness in every
                                        Japanese woman's
obi,
          his spermatophores travel down his arm and ejaculate
                                        his brightness
into her! The octopus sun, watery tongue moving contraction into
cankered corners of my myth, healthy corners, numb and
                                        lotus corners,
into nested mercy superior to its alternative 1000 years ago,

the Japanese claw of obedience so fearful Kannon a cool repose for
a candle and a few alms, who could want to take that away from
the
sex-terrified monk who stripped in 1955 testified against McCarthy
while I was a young guy in Phi Delta Theta an ant compared to
that monk
who placed 1001 Kannon into that sledge crossed night
So does it contract or stay in world movement static?

Scales seem to rave from fish now
given the form Mercury has assumed,
"the pansie freakt with jet"
We do not come from a greater or
go toward a greater. If you watch solely nature
sooner or later the limbs will clear into diapers, the leaves
will still show luminescent green over the fig
So we turn back indoors
rain splot outside
no crack to slip resolution through given a male
desire for eternity
Essential to in poetry destroy
his citadel dedicated to her
Your dove will fly
not solely toward a mast,
in upheaval will be perched
in the dovecot sterile yet
saddled with ticks, as if anything could define
what we feel embracing
finding we are all eyes in the chalk stem.

FULL PARTICULARS

M. D. ELEVITCH

> "Give full particulars . . ."
> —*The Agency*

Fresh from the corridor, this man arrived. Drops fell away; he quickly sat on the edge of the first chair, stretching the slippery raincoat, his knees protruding like prongs. He mashed his umbrella together and wedged it straight up between them.

SURNAME

Yes. He was elated. The receptionist's head bobbed above the desk to his right. She announced him promptly. Who had he come to. He had come to see. She was a green wire. She would send him.

The blood girl. His umbrella tipped, perilously, slicing the narrow room. She was beyond the low table at its center, startling, immaculate, her glossy red coat deployed in ample folds about a red, knitted lap. She wore—one thrust against the table—black, chunky platform boots. Her hair fell russet and rich from a center part like twin leaves; twin points glowed on cheekbones both delicate and severe. She had elevated her face; the mouthline arched sharply; on her lowered lids were thin, gold streaks. She had nothing further to declare. But at once she groaned sulkily, churned her hips, sagged back . . . Her inner humid siftings disturbed him, the red, unspilled blood. She was sprawling on a shrinking couch overcharged by an impossible balance of fragility and heat. He had the intercession of the nerve.

SURNAME

He accepted. He was Surname. She was nerve, she bounded up with a lump over her left glazed eye. Too many messages, the switchboard again, she was knotting them in her head, not long on the job, by this time she would have run out of storage space, they would have gone below, knobbing the knees, the ankles.

No, she knew how to discharge them, elsewhere, among other recipients. There was a screen and a door behind it for her to run through. And in the interim red girl with light, gold-nailed hand reached into the red and massaged it with muted, disdainful relief. Surname felt the rain at his thighs, high on his temples. Their smiles sparked in complicity. The receptionist returned.

LAST ADDRESS

It was growing familiar. There were old coffee cups and rubbed-out cigarettes on the low black table before him, he saw them as many completions, a residue of what decisions . . . Was he to speculate upon it or was he to withdraw the white envelope in his slicker and lay it as a renewal on those ashes . . .

LAST ADDRESS

The walls were dark, lined with posters, makeshift, indistinct, but somehow, from where he sat, their overlappings began to take form. They made him alert. Behind the desk he saw a lion. He started, creature of the lair, subjected to what must have been outlandish whimsy. No wonder the receptionist had gathered those knots. It was a giant, kindly, roaring lion head. This was a paper kingdom. New Britannia. Ancient breath in the room hurrying them on . . .

OCCUPATION

Pages cracked. A woman leapt, fresh from the corridor, headed for lion. But she stopped at his knees, cheerful, husky, offering tea or coffee, she assured him. Surname dismounted his umbrella and followed. She was a stewardess with authority to defy the blood. She might have been bone. No, she was flesh, her rapid rump joggling her jeans. They reached her alcove. She gave him plump elbows, at work on the drink.

OCCUPATION

He rushed. Up and down the hall, lion pacer, more posters distracting him, varied nude animals with winning, uncomplicated smiles, dimly visible in purple light. He approached the door, left ajar. She'd be just inside. She would have slid in his absence across the table, her scorching legs on his vacated, damp chair, her languid arms on the nerve woman at the desk, her mournful, taut jaw upturned and beginning to shatter the wall.

Tea summoned him. It was afternoon fitness, Cheer had decided, they would have it upstairs, she was ready with sugar and cream. Her voice was piping, her eyes rolled darkly. He postulated milk. She'd agree. She was Billingham, nurse of tea, her aroma was tea, she squeezed it from her armpits. That was her power. Tea put the damper on flame.

OCCUPATION

Surname came away on her promise. He was seized by thirst, a new intrusion enough to make him moan. A little milk, please. They charged, with loud clumps, winding, sloping tower stairs. She apologized joyfully for the disorder. Behind them now, the improvements, remedies, doors to rotate, locks to change, engineers everywhere, in baggy coveralls, where had he been, why hadn't he seen them. The brooms, wire coils, carpet rolls, the painters. Their putty lumps were wonders, their brushes ravenous! Her exclamations rang and echoed. They had flecks of white paint on their lashes! Sturdily she advanced the high candlestick cups of tea, steam curling back to drench his face. He sucked it fiercely, eyeing her elbow teats. Their breathing grew rapid, giddy; they were at the top. Billingham pushed ahead, transferred him with a brisk introduction, and put him to the test.

REFERENCES

"My eyes are red because I use my blood for looking. In this way, body certainties direct me and intelligence will become infallible as instinct."

"Did you say that again?"

"Did I?"

"Would you—"

This was Hilary. They were in the loftiest room, conversation was beginning . . . The ceiling, almost totally a skylight, slanted steeply down behind her. She sat erectly in a white suit, elbows at her sides, her fingers composed before her, a pencil between the middle knuckles with a black, smoldering eraser as though she had smoked it. She did seem rather befogged. Her shoulders were pinched, leaning imperceptibly toward a soaring, creamy neck, a heart head; somber blue eyes.

"Your eyes are embers."

"Not really. Let's say they're open for discussion. I was quoting a Chilean mystic of tender years."

Surname again found himself at the edge of a chair, this one extraordinarily large, the shape of a suppliant palm, padded and white. It was the only excess in the bare dormer. The desk was scratched and worn, its brown varnish fading; the telephone an isolated mound. He tore aside his rain gear, letting it fall. He nudged the white envelope onto the desk between the untouched cups of tea.

Hilary's gaze had locked beyond him. Because they sat at different levels and she was tall, he addressed the soft, pulsating tuck of flesh beneath her chin.

"You have an irresistible skylight above you."

"In the sense that—"

"In the sense that you are too hot in summer and too cold in winter. This is an elemental room."

"Your bloody eyes saw that?"

"I was quoting an Andean sprite. I consider Tufty Tails an abomination. They are wheeled about in carts by determined mothers."

"Why should that occur to you up here?" She slowly slipped long fingers about his envelope.

"Tufty Tails occur in packages carefully designed to fit those carts. Tufty Tails pinned on infants eliminates knowledge of their bubbly, reeking waste. The fact that Tufty Tail is completely and effortlessly discarded reinforces prejudice against this matter. In my estimation Tufty Tail will be made palatable to encourage infant to process prediapered sewage . . ."

But it was possible the light of the room was too harsh for him. The phone rang; she answered immediately; he settled back with a long sigh of torpid tea. She spoke in a very straight, regulated manner, assessing what she heard, it was all sorted out, she didn't see it as tufty tail so highly absorbent to blood. She continued with the phone, but took three pages from his envelope and set them on the desk.

REFERENCES

Wallaby entered swiftly, whirling to slap open a slatted folding chair which quickly creaked beneath him. He was lip, smiling perpetually under shiny, frameless glasses, strands of maizey hair swaying at his sideburns and untidy fringe of beard. His lip hung over a lip-colored sweatshirt, his belly creasing into another lip as he lounged forward. Hilary concluded her phone.

Surname paled under Wallaby's beaming. He gestured at his pages. If they too were gaping, strangely blanched, empty of content, that was an advantage, so said Surname, they could be interchanged, according to emphasis. Upside down, they would not lose intensity.

Wallaby listened, nodding amiably. He saw nothing to conflict with this newly minted evidence. He splayed his blunt fingers on his knee and ponderously pushed himself upright, still gazing at the curious exhibit from afar. A loose compilation, whatever was at hand, Surname rallied, it was enough to begin.

"We shall get you a photograph. That would be first."

"Multiply and be blessed. You have a Xerox."

"Needless to say. And we shall want to quote you."

SPECIAL INTERESTS

"There's one thing more—"

Surname felt directed. This easeful man was greasing his way. Anything, he had seen what they could do, he need only envision it, computers, a sauna, dispensers for scented paper towels . . . A mattress, forty-seven feet long, imagine it, for meditation, they would have it, if they must bring it through the roof.

"That's a helpful skylight."

"Very."

A skylight trap door, the idea was exalting, upward they looked, clearing their throats, runnels of rain spreading soundlessly on the gray glass. Wallaby and Surname wandered to the door. Hilary, with a ceremonious head-bow, took her tea. They would want to see him, in new offices, once the engineers had cleared. Wallaby's fuzzy cheek was moist under the glasses. Surname warmed. Wallaby chuckled, did he like lager, he must try it with lime, that was the way to do it. Do it? What was being offered—an improvement? A remedy for constipation? Hilary snapped back in her column.

SPECIAL INTERESTS

He was led deftly through an unknown passage to the elevator cage. In the freshly painted light blue hall its heavy golden bars shown crudely ornate, Wallaby's mauve sweatshirt bunching about them as he leaned to the button. His thumb drew a grunt from deep in the shaft. The box rose, gasping and grinding, at its top a lone, ragged cigarette tip to catch and hold their eyes. Flung down, obviously, in impatience. Wallaby was irritated. The cables were old, no need to flaunt it, the offensive fragment would need sweeping up, however difficult to reach. But it was there and, if Wallaby was to be believed, it would be eradicated.

"I believe you."

SPECIAL INTERESTS

Surname described the girl. He rambled, his excitement increasing as the lift approached; he had intended to return to her. The insufferable climb continued and finally halted with a crunch. Wallaby stood by firmly, sopping up Surname's discomfort. He pressed up breathlessly close, projecting brown, magnified eyes:

"Did she have red hair? I'll find out who she is and let you know."

SIGNATURE

Wallaby swung the outer door, slammed back the heavy folding one and started him downward. Surname absently hugged his stark coverings, his umbrella, the raincoat. He had left them his envelope. He watched as he descended his shadow rippling over the skyblue carpet on the surrounding stairs. He hadn't touched the button—Wallaby had determined his stop. He vacated quickly.

SIGNATURE

Now he was outside, dazzled, on the upper side of Knightsbridge, London, that year. He thought he saw in the distance a sheltering arcade. The traffic came in irregular screeching patterns, blasting him with wind and choking exhaust, holding him in place. A lancing rain started him again. His capillaries flexed, he had unlimited mileage. He brought up the umbrella. The curve of its rough, cherry-wood handle, held high, became for him a lean and sanguine face. On the street before him were giant letters printed in white. LOOK RIGHT. His look was right. He stepped forth at high speed. He was met by the shield of a Jensen Interceptor III K '71. Burgundy with cream hide interior. Sun-Dym glass. Refrigeration. Sixteen thousand miles. Superb condition.

She smiled. There was no shield, there was blood. Her condition was blood. She had opened her legs so many centimeters to the glorious tufty tap, and there in her corridor, in aching bursts of savage, dire joy, this man arrived.

SEVEN POEMS

A selection from *In Love and Death*

DACHINE RAINER

In memoriam, E. J. Ballantine

IN DEFENSE OF GAINSBOROUGH

From anywhere I see, the land might be Eighteenth Century, alder
and the willow hung river, cows grazing at their reflections
through the still, narcissistic day. Long legged water flies that hum
above the waterlilied stream. Blue day that belongs to the
                                                        bright heron.
Gainsborough's introspective cows, his romantically flung
                                                        trees design
a previous century. To my left, the sheep cropped pasture. On the
                                                        land's edge,
stiff marsh grasses, in the forefields patterned hayfields

sheep nibbled hedges . . . remote lavender hills . . . A white
owl flies through the deepened pink dusk, so low
above a field of black faced sheep it floats, sails, so near
my quiet brown eyes, huge before me in the long grass
like the pale ghost of an amorphous sheep. Above, the unmoving
                                                        sky
's natural structures of perpetuity. Before me this river
beneath a miniature bridge from fields to English fields

moves slow, green beneath Constable clouded heaven. It could
have been
imagined by Bonington or like our house, medieval (with
my small unobtrusive person who becomes Ur Kentishman, iron
aged Pict, pre-Roman or two thousand years before Christ)
flow back:
defying absurd teleology—as history deteriorates all
Marxian notion
of progress. Behind me this heavy century lies heaped upon
my back:
huge, senseless machines plow up distraught black fields, murder

living hedges, dismember continuity. Pastureless industry:
corrugated
mobs of maddened cattle brutally fattened for an all too
common profit
while old England's poor return to worried bread, sugary red jams
and dripping.
Ah! a marvel of small birds, frightened in the thickening
air, diminishing fish gulping their dense chemistry, this
River Eden
infiltrates a clump of nettlebedded bank tiding my century
's uneasy perceptions, whose acid deaths corrode my bones, disrupt
my dreams.

DOUBLE TOMB

On our high ritual anniversary
(counting marriage from that instant
our matched vision struck fire) ceremonially
you had noted: *poets should always be in love.*

Remember when I'm gone
that it won't much matter
me or any other. Bravery
(disbelieving him) or romantic irony.

But you, ever gravely
responsive to my incredulity:
(how could this
each solitary oneness be us?)

Showed, although wrapt in sensuality,
concern for our post mythical time:
Remember, without love
and therefore without poetry, you'll be

a dead, dull feathered duck; a wild
blind cuckoo, distraught; he warned,
remember to love. I remembering his smile
apparitional, a musical quaver . . . as the child

separated from us both remembers each (like
an amputee an approximation of the function of his leg) finds
nothing remaining of love but habit which demands
a distant image to cook for, to bed down.

He meant, when he said "love," love, I knew,
not sex presumptively (which nonetheless suffused us
with its clear glow: *Something marvellous*
must be happening to you! cried an acquaintance, stepping
                                                    beside us.)

Any carpet slippered view of him never ceased to stir me
by his elegant, aging beauty, and that gay, graceful, mellifluous
speech so prompt at camouflaging wisdom: *Don't let on,*
you're happy, Sybarite; you'll tempt fate.

I make these poems for a rotting corpse in Highgate.
I had laughed, deeply sensuous as any contented temptress;
You'll look like a Rubens, excessive!
our laughter outside the gravitational stress

of fate. But my figure has lost
its pastel light and Renoir form
to a greying Rembrandt bathwoman
paddling about the motionless tomb

of once home. Twenty-one months
(the ponderous gestation of an elephant)
and I am unreconciled to every
clumsy dance with life in an emptied world.

This poem is for a rotting corpse in Highgate
and for myself, for whom
the nearby earth, below, above, surrounding him,
must only a little longer, unstirred, wait.

EN ROUTE TO ESSEN

One man, one child, one dog, one self and one's undivided
attention:
I belong to the great tradition of poets, those who loathed
travelling,
having abandoned nomadic tradition centuries past were rooted
in croft
and outlying pasture no further, who might, like Pascal, say: All
the trouble
in the world comes of man being unable to stay in one room
with one other, one child one dog and the self's fulfilling

concentration. Instead, that final Buster Keaton scene, our
hearts parting
in front of Lloyd's Sloane Square, combating the tragic with
the ludicrous
the dog in tears and I heroic in a mute animal way
walking off in opposite directions, pistols cocked.
Betrayed, what have either of us in common with
the baffling human or henceforth with any kind of love?

When I leave England and my heart and other remains in that
hillside grave
so near George Eliot, with accidental hideousness so near Karl Marx
(*three Jews*—he said once, looking dubiously at my Jewish
soul, teasingly

forgiving, with grace—*will have done in the entire evolutionary
process.*)
That grave waits so intently on my diminishing; the man
the dog and my divided self, each absent from custom and place.

Loved Child, towards whom in this Christmas season I move,
profusion
is unsettling. In nature, intensity requires singleness and
living form:
a white tea rose rather than abundance of floribunda in every shade
of yellow/red; this aimless century's mobile affluence full cycle
with technological error's invention, African exempt, of the wheel.
Beyond a crude spoon and rock civilization the bomb proliferates.
I think of
the man, child, dog, my self once fulfilled, nature's simplest
generosities
as wheels jolt and scream gyrating separation from leaping car
to car
on the frenetic sleeper to Bruxelles. On morning's windswept
wet station
guitar ornamented wildhaired crowds swoop like vocal flocks
of birds disoriented by hurricane. What do you see when you
travel? I ask
a rucksack bearer. *People.* Have you no people in Bruxelles?
I think of Pascal;

how it takes one entire lifetime to understand one cannot know
oneself . . . one's man, child, dog, one's—*ripeness is all*—
only self.
When I greet my-no-longer-Child, daughter, elsewhere, I remain
foreign
despite my best German for the occasion of her first man; a stranger
in this long vacation from recognition, I begin craving England
one man, one child, one dog, my self, my grave and home.

A DEVOTIONAL

1

Midwinter surrounds our historic Kent house
reluctant to have its history enlarged by us.

Nearly March, a local snow of abrupt vigor
thrusts the winter backwards towards its center.

A boldly frilled wind promenades the heaviest beam
of this vast, Thirteenth Century bedroom

where I am in bed, wishing I had
of royal purple stuff thick bedcurtains against the draft.

2

I am protected by your drawings, surrounding me on three walls
timber framed landscapes, live form of the nudes, a classical

nude-in-landscape, reminding how once for love you
                                        bettered Giorgione,
a child's sleeping head, pastel lovers . . . and before me

the lad's careful fire now blazing logs, a devotional
stack high and deep against the whitened chimney wall.

Heaped upon the bed Cummings' and Ford's poems and within
                                        my heart,
Nelly Sachs' and Möricke's, the quartet

tumbled against my thigh, sharing my pillow and my heart;
my heart, such accumulated gifts, turbulence

tragedies and unfinished work teasing resistance
to despair, mocking indolence.

3

Downstairs an ignorant, innocent, tall youth
in the hot, protected inglenook,

reads *Anna Karenina* (an unexpected, late blessing;
I am grateful to quixotic Providence). Marvelling,

he sighs, with excess, returns to Hudson's rural scenes.
I lie in bed, wishing I were a Colette heroine:

that is, not too old for a young man . . . but I am.
Sensual still, perhaps, but no beauty remains

(extravagantly sustained in one unrenewable lacquered passion)
. . . yet not old enough to lose interest this abruptly.

Our grey Blue Point cat, imperious Fred, is listening to Callas
                                                    and Gobbi
and purring approval. I should be safe as Neanderthal's wife in
                                                    a cave.

Fred's claw slyly seizes an old drawing pencil—yours—
I have futilely captured for my listless hand. He bites

gently to warn me that more people that I love are dead.
I count the living quickly, a short list: below

I almost hear the young man stretch his thin frame, to call "Fred."
My heart, the unrelieved mourning dove of a devoted widow.

I think of Titan, with a young love and Minna with aged Goethe,
I consider Ford, breathless in Provence, with blessed barefoot
                                                    Schenehaia,

a final treat: gardening, writing, painting; like our marriage, a
                                                    late night heat;
I am abandoned by the dead. All else is unseemly. Besides, it
                                                    requires rapport

with God's blessings, a *Buckshee* I have never had;
and last, I think of Sappho . . . leaping into space instead.

TORCELLO: THE EARLIER VENICE

"In despair seize love"—Laura Riding

1

We had our picnic in the penetrating January rain
sheltering on marble steps overhung by parabolas
of vaulting Basilico: on marble steps edged by wet grass
and small desultory drops of jewelled rain on the lawn;
when one is young—one of us is—and in love, that is what one does.

The smoke hurtling spume curling vaporetti had released us
at the island and departed, leaving us attended
by that translucent silence peculiar to Torcello.
In its plagued reminder, its mysterious remains of rural splendor
we walked under our dark umbrella on grassy paths towards
                                                    Byzantium.

A civilizations's mosaic touchstones in dome and pink tower.
After wine and bread—coarse Tuscan wine and a narrow crusty
                                                    loaf—
crisp apples and a few soft green figs, incredulous,
I could live on this, he muttered, nothing else.
—and love and love (my thought stiff, smiling, ecstatic as worship).

We shared our picnic with two Torcellan country cats
—Tabby and a White—who overcame fear to lick roughly
a small dab of butter off the tip of his inviting finger; fiercely,
the less selective Tabby ate the bread as well.
Rats, they must live off rats, he said softly,

masking pity ineffectually: butter baited half grown Tabby
could be lured to have her back stroked; we see her sensuous
in our red tiled Inglenook before Western civilization in flames
on her side, on the other, on her back, stroked.
You prefer cats to women? Guilelessly. *More of them are beautiful.*

Relaxed from hunger, we played in once plague consumed Torcello
while several ceramic pots, an urn on the broken lawn
and the weather mutilated vivid marbles watched
the antic English. A monk paced by amazed. *This
had been what Venice is,* we marvelled, whispering

to each other, senselessly happy in the stillness among
the pink ruins, green, grey Byzantine protection vaulting above
like primitive angels greedy with love. He said,
I prefer it, appreciating grass beneath his feet,
and simple with prophecy: *This is what Venice will become.*

2

That evening, his long thick hair streaming
after a thoughtful walk in the cobbled Venetian rain,
his long pale face immobile, he sat dreaming

looking out across the moving canal at the Guidecca,
rolling a smoke, his long quick fingers tumbled my mind.
Unknowing how to say what I mean, I dared hope he'd remain

throughout the misted night's soft pattering
and the noisy undulating unspoken constant passion
between canals, lagoon and the too coldly battered stones of Venice.

Instead: *This is the first time man has chosen self-
destruction consciously,* I said, furiously distorting our mood
(as though this monstrous choice was for his gentle mind).

You think I do not care? He stared scornfully,
despising expression of the obvious: one knows what one knows
and too simple to know my qualms, he arose quickly. All night

the rain continued to cruise the islands as though on a voyage
                                                    of discovery,
knowing what small winds to ride, how turbulence to advantage,
                                what favours of sleep to grant,
while Venice inched itself a little uncertainly deeper into the sea.

WHITSUN, HYDE PARK

I am an old woman aimless on a warm park bench falling
asleep with a dead husband (no American strain
would graft on my European heart
as readily this British widowhood)
Before me the orange sail Serpentine dozing
and the iridescent heads of drake ducking
and drifting. My lonely dog at my feet dreaming of these
with noticeable alacrity but to no useful purpose,
starts—and subsides, and again starts and heaves
her large self into a labouriously lazy semi-recline
to view the scrambling pigeons with companionable pity,

and disdain.

HIGHGATE CEMETERY, FIVE YEARS AFTER

Rooted in earth, as once I was with you above . . .
detained here at the cemetery's massive gate, the porter
leering, impatient keys jangling iron five to five locked
two tones below the recurrent crash of delayed thunder
sparse drops of desolating rain splashing down to earth
where once I was rooted, with you above, sky to my adoring eyes.

Restrained from our grave these few particles of remaining me,
their wild imaginings: the whole affection of your arms, pressure
of your lips, your words uprooting my authoritative heart
here your tumbled torse, graceful legs and all between
elegance and that fire on earth where often you walked
with me, the tentative sky adoring us. Bound over, jailed

to my unwanted body I know the stunning pain within
my scooped out heart that hollow in which
like roosting pigeons our love's at home, imprisoned
by grass and trees and clouds and hills, our half-tenanted
grave, and this locked gate between your death and me. My passage
to your bed: I expect no faltering love above, no stumbling

love beneath

this earth. Sky to my adoring eyes, you above the savaged
                                        afternoon, lightning spurs
the doomed clouds over cemetery walls into the neighboring park
where see us in unrelated procession: me, barefoot, wet
                                        and wildhaired,
our large dog gifted with frenetic liberation chasing a
                                        frightened drake,
and the youth whose eyes are not so innocent of winter as one
                                        might hope
beneath this heaving sky, this earth, companions to my death.

NOTES ON CONTRIBUTORS

A frequent contributor to the New Directions anthologies, WALTER ABISH has also published extensively in literary magazines, among them *TriQuarterly, Paris Review, Fiction, Confrontation,* and *Statements: New Fiction.* His books include the novel *Alphabetical Africa* (1974); a collection of short fiction, *Minds Meet* (1975); and *Duel Site* (1970), a volume of poetry.

A prominent figure in modern Turkish literature, MELIH CEVDET ANDAY's work has been published in Europe, the Soviet Union, England, and the United States. A recipient of many literary awards, he enjoys fame as a playwright, novelist, essayist, translator, critic, and poet. BRIAN SWANN's fictions, *Liking the Sky,* were published earlier this year by Latitudes Press, and his translations of Tristan Tzara, *Primele Poeme/First Poems,* are soon to appear from New Rivers Press. His co-translator, TALAT SAIT HALMAN, is currently a professor of Turkish studies at Princeton University.

MARTIN BAX's "The Syndrome of Gilles de la Tourette" is excerpted from the novel *The Trials of Sir Maximov Flint.* As yet unpublished, it is the sequel to *The Hospital Ship,* brought out by New Directions this fall. The author, who lives in London, is a practicing physician and also edits the British literary periodical *Ambit.*

The author of *A ZBC of Ezra Pound,* CHRISTINE BROOKE-ROSE lectures in linguistics at the University of Paris, Vincennes. Her structuralist analysis of Pound's "Usura" Canto has been published by Mouton in Holland, and Hamish Hamilton, Ltd., London, has published her novels *Between, Such, Out,* and, most recently, *Thru.*

FREDERICK BUSCH's *Domestic Particulars,* a fictional family chronicle in thirteen episodes, has just been published by New Directions. A regular contributor to these pages, he is the author of a critical study *Hawkes: A Guide to His Fictions* (1973) and last spring participated in a Hawkes symposium at Muhlenberg College in Allentown, Pennsylvania. "George Dolby, or The Cannibal Sheep" is the opening chapter of *The Inimitable,* Busch's current work-in-progress.

An excerpt from COLEMAN DOWELL's first novel, *One of the Children Is Crying* (Random House), recently appeared in *Kentucky Renaissance: An Anthology of Contemporary Writing* (Gnomon Press), edited by Jonathan Greene. New Directions has published two of his novels to date, *Mrs. October Was Here* (1974) and *Island People* (1976). His fourth book, *Too Much Flesh and Jabez,* will appear in the near future.

Born in Minnesota, M. D. ELEVITCH has contributed fiction and articles to numerous magazines, newspapers, and anthologies. His novel, *Grips, or Efforts to Revive the Host* was published by Grossman in 1972, and *Americans at Home* appeared under the First Person imprint this spring.

CLAYTON ESHLEMAN has published numerous volumes of poetry, most recently *The Gull Wall* (Black Sparrow Press, 1976). His translation of Vallejo's *Poemas Humanos* (1968) was published by Grove Press. The former editor of *Caterpillar* magazine, he now resides in Los Angeles.

GAVIN EWART's first book of poems, *New Verse,* appeared in 1933. Since then he has published seven additional volumes of poetry, including *Pleasures of the Flesh* (1966), *The Gavin Ewart Show* (1971), and *No Fool Like an Old Fool* (1976). Educated at Wellington College and Christ's College, Cambridge, he has served in the Royal Artillery and presently resides in London, where he is a free-lance writer and part-time teacher of English.

The poet, novelist, and radio-playwright RÜDIGER KREMER was born in Schwerte (West Germany) and has been an editor for Radio-Bremen. His monologue "The List" (*Die liste der ernährten*) was included in *ND27,* translated by BREON MITCHELL, whose *James Joyce and the German Novel* was published in 1976 by Ohio University Press.

Information on the "Four Australian Poets" BRUCE DAVIE, WILLIAM FLEMING, LES A. MURRAY, and GRACE PERRY, will be found in the note preceding their work. NOEL STOCK, who made this selection, formerly edited *Edge,* one of the leading Australian literary journals, before joining Ezra Pound in Italy. Now the American representative for *Poetry Australia,* he teaches at the University of Toledo in Ohio. He has written a major biography of Pound, as well as several critical books and articles on the poet.

THOMAS MERTON, whose first book of poems appeared under the New Directions imprint in 1944, died in December 1968, in Bangkok, Thailand, where he was attending a conference on monasticism. His *Collected Poems,* which will be published in the near future, contains all the poetry from his published books, plus appendixes of uncollected and previously unpublished poetry and translations. His "Four Uncollected Poems" are taken from the material the editors found in assembling the late Trappist monk's work.

A landscape architect who now operates a construction business in connection with a community storefront on Manhattan's Lower East Side, ROBERT NICHOLS was born in Worcester, Massachusetts, in 1919. He left home at an early age to travel extensively throughout Europe and the United States. At times he was "accomplice" to his father's lengthy train journeys across this continent, and in *Slow Newsreel of Man Riding Train* (City Lights, 1962) he recounts some of his father's adventures. He has been writing a sequel to *Daily Lives in Nghsi-Altai,* and this past spring published a book of poems and prints with Lucia Vernarelli, *Address to the Smaller Animals* (Penny Each Press).

American by birth, DACHINE RAINER became a British subject on July 19, 1975. Her recent novella *Copper Coloured* was inspired by the numerous visits from Scotland Yard detectives investigating her citizenship application. The widow of E. J. Ballantine, the Scottish sculptor, actor-director, and founder of the Provincetown Players, she has been widely published in magazines and anthologies, including *ND12* and *ND26.* She writes that her more serious work of late, besides poetry, includes a "little book of memoir and appreciation of e e cummings."

JEROME ROTHENBERG has published over a dozen volumes of poetry and translated several works from both the German and Seneca languages. He co-edits, with Dennis Tedlock, *Alcheringa,* a journal of ethnopoetics. In 1975 New Directions reissued his *Poems for the Game of Silence,* after having published *Poland/1931,* a continuing series of "ancestral" poems. He is now completing *A Big Jewish Book: Poems & Other Visions of the Jews from Tribal Times to the Present,* a new work in the mode of his revolutionary anthologies, *Technicians of the Sacred* and *Shaking the Pumpkin.* His *Seneca Journal* will appear from New Directions in the near future.

ARAM SAROYAN lives in Bolinas, California, with his wife Gailyn, a painter and writer, and their two daughters, Strawberry and Cream. His published books include *Pages* (Random House), *Words & Photographs* (Big Table), *Poems* (Telegraph), and an autobiographical novel called *The Street* (Bookstore Press). He is now at work on a book of critical pieces, tentatively titled *The Human Community: American Writing in the Seventies.*

PAUL WEST has published more than ten books of fiction, criticism, and general prose. *Gala,* sequel to *Words for a Deaf Daughter* (Harper & Row, 1970), is scheduled for this fall. He has previously contributed stories to *ND28* and *ND31.*

Director of science and research policy in the Ministry of Planning, Burma, U WIN PE, writes a weekly column on science for a leading Rangoon daily. He has published a book of translations into English from the classical Burmese and is a leading member of the movement to modernize his country's poetry. Author of *Rythmn and Image,* a study of Burmese verse, he has also written on Theravada Buddhist meditation.

Recent fiction by WILLIAM S. WILSON has appeared in *Antaeus* and *TriQuarterly,* and his critical writings have been published in *Arts* magazine. *Antaeus* has also published his long essay on the word *energy,* "where love may now be sheer energy of attention".

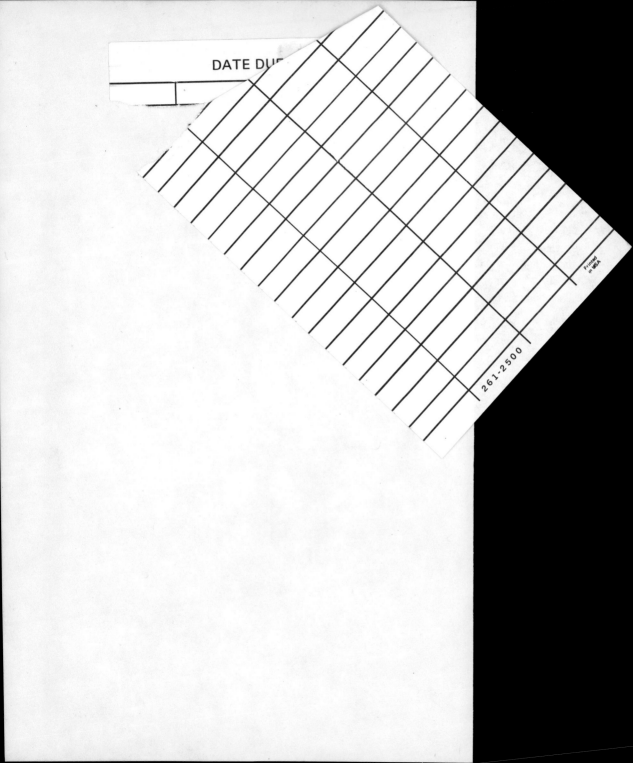

DATE DUE

261-2500

Printed
in USA